THE DISCARDED

A HORROR NOVEL

JERRY BLAZE

BAYNAM BOOKS PRESS

Copyright © 2025 by Jerry Blaze

All rights reserved.

No portion of this book may be reproduced in any form without written permission from the publisher or author, except as permitted by U.S. copyright law.

The story, its characters, and incidents portrayed in this work are fictitious. No identification with actual persons (living or deceased), places, buildings, and products is intended or should be inferred.

This book contains scenes of graphic horror, SA, intense gore and much more. Reader discretion is advised.

Cover art by Adrian Medina.

SOME BOOKS BY JERRY BLAZE

Jerry Blaze is the author of over 60 titles, below is a sampling of some of his favorite works.

Flakka Ferret Frenzy

Deadly Seed

Arachnicunt

Deadly Seed 2

Carnage

Knightmare!

Blood on the Prairie

The Honkening

Beaver's Bend Bloodbath

Cannibal Cruise

For Mom,

Who has always believed in me.

Contents

Introduction by Dan Shrader

There are books that entertain.

There are books that disturb.

Then there's The Discarded—a brutal plunge into humanity's darkest depths. Blood, bile, and brilliance stain every page. This isn't sanitized horror; this is the raw, unflinching truth.

This story follows two monsters on a collision course—one wears a lab coat, the other hides behind a suburban smile. And you, lucky reader, are about to watch it all unfold. Thanks to Jerry Blaze.

Who is Jerry Blaze?

He's the type of author who feeds you his filth soaked in gasoline and then sets your conscience on fire!

He's an international bestselling author of extreme horror and Bizarro fiction, with breakout titles like *Killer Nose Candy*, *Deadly Seed*, and *Arachnicunt*. And that is just naming a tiny fraction of his work. The dude has written a lot of books. I mean a shit ton!

After dominating the erotic-horror scene, Blaze shifted to full-bore splatterpunk, earning the bestseller status on Amazon and picking up the Golden Wizard Book Prize and the Literary Titan Award in 2025. The guy bleeds Grindhouse and exploitation cinema, and every page reflects that '70s/'80s fuck-you energy that made the genre infamous.

But The Discarded? Yes, let's get back to this one. That's why we're all here, right? This is a whole new beast.

This book is Jerry's most brutal and soul-rotting achievement yet. It's not just shock for shock's sake—it's a double-barreled shotgun blast to the face. It's sprinkled with all the wonderful horror tropes of science, serial murder, psychosexual obsession, and a city too numb to care.

If you're a fan of his earlier freakshows—strap in. This is deeper. Sicker. More emotionally broken.

Blaze has outdone himself with The Discarded. It's not just another splatterfest—it's a statement. A hellish, thought-provoking, skin-crawling work of modern horror that shows us what happens when society throws its sins in the trash...

...and what crawls back out.

Brace yourself. This one's gonna leave a stain.

Dan Shrader

06/11/2025

PROLOGUE

The truck slowly pulled up to the driveway of the building and proceeded to creep around toward the back. The building was the local abortion clinic, and at this late hour, it was closed for the night. The driver parked the vehicle and shut off the engine, leaving the key in the ignition.

After opening the glovebox, he reached in and pulled on a pair of leather gloves that had seen better days. Making sure they were velcroed tightly around his wrists to prevent slippage, he wrenched open the door and exited the large vehicle. He was a bigger man with a bulky presence and a ball cap concealing his face from any cameras that might be focusing on the area.

Walking around to the back of the truck, he unlatched and threw up the metal door to prepare for the next phase of his operation. Upon revealing the contents of his travel trailer, he reached in and grabbed a large plastic container with its lid sealed, along with the dolly to wheel it to and from the next destinations.

Whistling a soft tune on his cracked lips, he started toward the dumpster that was located next to the chain-link fence that went around the building. He had a job to do, and it needed to be done with care; otherwise, he'd kiss his payment goodbye. He'd been all over the city, picking up what he could and gathering whatever else he'd hoped to find, marking off locations on his list as he went about.

Stopping as he reached the dumpster, he felt in his pocket and pulled out a face mask to apply over his nose and mouth; the last thing he wanted was the stench of the contents to attach itself to his senses.

Prying open the lid of the container, the man walked up to the dumpster and lifted the heavy black top until he could see inside. Immediately, the foul odor escaped from within and blew into the air around him. He pulled away to cough and gag furiously as he caught a whiff from the sides of the mask. It was absolutely putrid as a motherfucker.

He needed to double his rate for this shit.

Reaching into his coat pocket, he gripped the mini-flashlight and clicked it on, turning back to view the inside of the dumpster. He saw bags of blood and chunky contents within, along with various boxes marked with hazard signs and thousands of maggots crawling desperately over the remains of God's creations.

Turning away, he quickly lowered the mask and released a funnel of vomit onto the ground, upchucking all of his dinner from the greasy spoon up the street. *Goddamnit,* he thought.

Wiping his mouth with the sleeve of his jacket, he pulled the mask back over his mouth and nose before returning to his work. Reaching into the dumpster, he grabbed the top of one of the plastic bags and lifted it out, shining the light to see the floating remains within the fluid-filled bag, and set it down into the plastic container. Shaking his head, he turned back to the dumpster and reached in to tug on one of the boxes marked with a hazard stamp, only for the bag to tear apart from the wet remains within and flood the dumpster with the juices of God-knows-what.

Doing his best not to puke again, he held the flashlight in the dumpster and grabbed the corpse with his left hand before lifting it out of the large metal bin. Moving aside, he placed it into the plastic container and proceeded to do the same with another corpse he fished out of a similar box. He could feel his stomach burning with the urge to release another flood of leftovers, but he fought it back.

Fucking Christ.

Finally, he grabbed another bag of remains floating in a bag like some obscene fish won in a carnival game and placed it in the container. Coughing slightly in the mask, he pulled the lid to close on the dumpster and immediately replaced the cover on the container before ripping the mask off his face. The fresh air hit his nostrils, and he breathed a sigh of heavy relief.

There was no way he'd be back again. This job was wrong in every sense of the word. He already didn't like these places for their base inhumanity, but this was a step too far, and he was ready to call the boss to let him know he was retiring without pay.

But, then again, he did have child support payments eating at him, and he wasn't the most hireable person on earth, due to a criminal rap sheet a mile long. No, fuck it, he'd just keep plying his trade as best he could.

He had to make ends meet somehow or another. He'd do what needed to be done. Shaking his head, he popped a cigarette in his mouth and lit up before he started pushing the container on the dolly back toward the trailer on his truck. He was ready for the night to be done and over with. He didn't feel compelled to fish in any more dumpsters for the rest of the evening.

Especially since he already had three containers filled to the brim with the corpses of fetuses and toddlers.

Chapter One

The warehouse was a large brick building that was situated in a seedy part of the city, where it stood like a shadow of death over the smaller buildings on the lot. The building was dilapidated, and if the city had ever conducted a proper inspection, it would have been condemned for demolition.

Of course, that would mean the city would actually have to follow through with something, and that never happened. Most condemned buildings in the city tended to deteriorate naturally and collapse in on themselves. It was a tragedy, but nobody in the city council paid any attention to it.

However, this building had its uses, and its current owner was making full use of the large empty space within the warehouse interior. He was a scientist, and while he wasn't currently employed anywhere, he was working on something that would pay off in the long term. He had an idea that would prove to be super beneficial to mothers, both single and married, all over the world.

Walking back and forth between the two large tables that held numerous beakers, jars, and other instruments of scientific research, the scientist busied himself with mixing the various chemicals that he gathered through various enterprises. Taking a second to scratch his balding scalp, he let out a heavy sigh before mixing another small vial of liquid into the large beaker bubbling away within.

The idea had come to him in his sleep, and it struck him like a bolt of lightning from Beyond. Soon, he would be the toast of the town, the talk of elite social circles, and maybe he would even get his face on the cover of Time magazine or some fancy periodical. After all, who didn't want their infant to tell them why they were upset rather than screaming or crying or acting like a complete bastard?

Dr. Kermit Black certainly didn't know. Kids were not something he was fond of, nor did he have any interest in creating his own, but he knew that nobody liked a screaming infant that served as little more than a guessing game at what problem had befallen its frail little body. With his serum, he would be able to give parents everywhere the ability to get some real sleep, keep their shitty marriages complete, and help their kids with whatever trivial needs had caused them discomfort.

Licking his lips as he focused on the mixture in the beaker, the doctor was more than a little giddy over the accolades that danced in his brain.

Soon, a noise caught his attention, and he looked over his shoulder to spot his temporary helpers bringing in the shipment of secret supplies he had ordered. Smiling, he lifted two fingers to his mouth and whistled for their attention before gesturing where to place the boxes. The gruff and heavyset workers quietly marched toward the large table and placed the boxes in the open spaces they could find. Dr. Black tapped his fingertips together before walking over to examine the boxes.

They were sealed and marked **FRAGILE**, but he knew the contents were actually relatively sturdy. The label was to ensure they were handled with absolute care. Looking at the helpers, Dr. Black smiled. "Are there any more boxes to be brought in, or is this it?"

"Um—" the taller of the two looked at his partner and then back to the doctor before shaking his head. "No, I think this is it."

"Excellent," Dr. Black replied before reaching into his white lab coat and pulling out two wrinkled hundred-dollar bills. "Thank you for your assistance."

The men took their pay as the shorter of the two looked around at everything in the warehouse. Sniffing, he wiped his nose and looked back at the doctor. "So, what's all this for? Are you inventing some new kinda lip balm?"

Dr. Black laughed loud enough to make the two tremble slightly before shaking his head, "No. I'm working on something much bigger and better in the long run. However, if I told you, I'd have to kill you."

"Ooh, top secret?"

"Precisely," the doctor smiled before gesturing toward the door. "Now, run along, and if I need you again, I'll call."

"You got it," the larger of the two replied as they started to make their egress from the warehouse. It was a creepy place. The doctor was a creepy guy. Hell, the whole thing just left a bad feeling in their gut. They didn't trip over themselves as they got out of the warehouse, jumped into their delivery van and fucked off as another vehicle came rumbling up into the parking lot of the warehouse.

Meanwhile, Dr. Black reached into his dirty lab coat and pulled out a box cutter, using his thumb to press the switch to push the blade up enough for use. Looking at one of the boxes marked *'fragile,'* he pulled the blade along the top of the folds and sliced through the heavy tape that kept the box sealed.

Licking his lips, he set the knife down and pulled open the folds to revel in what the hunk of cardboard contained.

His eyes feasted upon the bags of goop that were near to bursting with volume. *Fuck,* he thought, this was easier than he'd ever thought it would be.

Reaching within, he pulled out one of the heavy bags and set it on the table, marveling over the brown, goopy liquid within the plastic bag. It was a proper ingredient that had cost more than a pretty penny, but money was no object when one was on the brink of a major scientific achievement. Said achievement would also pay for itself in massive dividends that would make it all worthwhile.

Nodding with a crooked grin, Doctor Black was more than satisfied with what his purchase had provided.

Soon, a rattling on the garage door of the warehouse caught his attention, and the doctor turned to hurry over toward it. His next delivery was in motion. It was all coming together for him.

Pressing the green button on the remote hanging beside the door, the heavy metal started rising from its resting place and revealed the outside beyond it. The doctor watched precariously as the door continued to lift high enough for a delivery truck to back up toward the opening.

Once it had risen far enough, Black released the button and moved to the center of the opening as he watched the travel trailer backing into the landing Raising his hand, he gestured for the driver to continue as far back as he could before signaling him to stop. The truck was parked and shut off before the driver exited the large vehicle. Black smiled as he placed his hands on his hips. "Did you get as much as you could?"

The driver walked up to the landing before climbing up to stand beside the doctor and nodded. "Yeah, I did, and by the way, this is the sickest shit I've ever been contracted to do. I want you to know I don't appreciate this kind of work."

"Oh?" Black cocked an uncaring eyebrow. "Do you prefer enforcer work? Breaking legs and collecting loans for small-time hoods? I'm giving you the chance to contribute to a Nobel Prize, and you're going to complain about it?"

"Well," the driver rubbed the back of his head and shrugged. "I'm just saying, fishing baby corpses out of a dump is just heinous compared to everyday work."

Black looked at the man and shook his head. *Fool*. He didn't understand that this was the kind of work animal labs did regularly. At least he wasn't being contracted to follow the original plan and kidnap living toddlers for the experiments. He'd like to tell the fucking grunt just how easy he actually had it, but he couldn't trust the man to not blab to the police, regardless of whether they found out just what he'd been doing all right. Besides, he still had one more need from the man.

Patting the driver on the shoulder, Black smiled, "Now, now; this is the last fishing job I have for you. Go ahead and unload your catches while I get your payment ready."

The driver shook his head before turning to open the back of the trailer. He stepped inside, getting the dolly ready to pull out the containers of material for the doctor's needs. The smell was putrid and emanating heavily from the inside of the trailer itself, but he didn't care at this point.

He was almost done.

The finish line was in sight.

Doctor Black walked over to the table that contained the lockbox where he kept his cash and fished the key out of his pocket, inserting it into the lock before twisting it open. Taking the lock off the box, he raised the lid and reached within to grab the payment for the driver, chuckling as he did. People were willing to do anything for money. It was almost absurd.

Turning to look over his shoulder, he watched as the driver wheeled the last of the heavy blue containers out of the trailer and next to the large table that served as a catch-all for the experiment materials. The driver pulled the dolly out from under the container and set it aside, wiping his hands as he turned toward the doctor.

Black looked back down at the lockbox. "So, did we agree on two grand or three?"

"Three."

"I thought so." Black nodded. "Oh, I have one more thing I need from you."

The driver sighed. He knew the doctor was going to ask for more work. He wasn't opposed to it, but at this point, it was getting ridiculous, and the work was growing more and more disturbing. Still, he'd like to be ahead of his child support payments and maybe even have a little leftover for his girlfriend. Money talked, after all.

Shrugging, the driver nodded. "Okay, what do you need?"

"I need a body."

"I just brought you three containers filled with bodies."

"No." Black shook his head, "I need an adult body."

The driver tilted his head. "You want me to go to the morgue?"

"Oh no, I need it fresh," the doctor replied before turning around with a .9mm raised in his right hand. Before the driver could react, Doctor Black pulled the trigger and sent a round directly into the driver's throat, forcing blood to run freely from the gaping wound down the front of his heavy jacket. The driver fell back onto the floor, gagging and gasping for air as he attempted to cover the wound with his meaty hands.

Black turned back to the table and placed the gun in his lockbox, focusing on his notes as he listened to the driver's wet grunts and struggling breaths fill the air until the gunshot did its job. It wouldn't be long, but he'd enjoy the sounds while they lasted, a little levity before the hard work began.

Sacrifices had to be made.

Chapter Two

The fog covered the city streets, the silence of the air punctuated by the sound of sirens in the distance, cars honking, and the occasional rumbling of the city tram going to its next location.

Henry Markoz was on the prowl.

He stalked through the shadows, dressed in his gray overcoat; he was bundled for the cold night on the town. He held the heavy metal tool in his inner coat pocket, snug against his chest, the constant weight reminding him of its presence. He was eager to skulk about in search of what he wanted.

His car was parked a few miles down in the parking lot outside of an office building. He'd paid the toll for the parking and knew it would be there for a few hours without any potential issue. He didn't need his car being towed for overstaying its welcome before he got back to it.

The chill of the air hit him as he moved swiftly through the alleys of the area, gliding through the darkness like a buyer sifting through potential commodities, eager to find the one he wanted. He saw her, a long-legged sex worker moving with ease between the city blocks and smoking long thin cigs, or slims as they were known. His eyes gazed at her body, thin and dressed in a revealing two-piece silk outfit that she'd tied in triple knots to ensure it held to her frame; a pair of sumptuous red stilettos adorned her feet.

He licked his lips as he watched her come down the sidewalk toward the alley where he was staying. He remained poised, eager, and willing to venture out when she had gone past him.

He breathed slowly, doing his best to keep from coughing from the remnants of the cold he'd suffered earlier that week. Getting sick was always a problem, and since he tended to spend his nights outside in the dank alleys of the city, he was nearly always catching a bug, but it was part of the game. She was walking by him, and he remained hidden, her face focused on the front path she took to walk to the next corner.

Apparently, she wasn't getting any customers tonight.

It was a dead area.

Probably full of junkies and rats hiding in the dark.

He was one of them. Not a junkie for the pipe or the needle, no, he was a junkie for more physical needs. Of course, her job was to satisfy those needs, but alas, his needs went a bit further.

He would still enjoy her. He needed to feel his release with her body. It wasn't as incredible as what he planned for what she had, but it was going to be enough to tide him over for now, and some things were more than they were worth. Yet, he continued with what he had to do because he loved it.

Like the taste of blood.

Licking his upper lip, he felt his tongue come into contact with a zit on the corner, and he sighed. He was in his mid-thirties and still getting acne, a product of the sugar he filled his body with. Unfortunately, sugar helped kill the cravings he got for more, and like most things in life, sugar was the benefactor of bad physical problems.

It was certainly not helping his weight gain.

Turning slightly out of the alley, he saw the woman walking across the road to the next corner and waiting for potential customers to come. However, the streets were barren beyond the bits of trash that blew about from the wind that popped up occasionally. It wasn't looking like she was going to be getting any customers anytime soon.

Exiting the alley, he walked along the sidewalk towards her, keeping his hands in his pockets as he went. The warmth was nice, but he wasn't interested in warmth; he was interested in something more.

Moving across the street, he made his way onto the next block, standing outside of a closed laundromat that made up most of the block itself. The woman, his target, looked over at him and said, "Hey, you need a date?"

"Huh?"

"Yeah," she smiled, striking a pose, "I can be your girlfriend tonight."

"Thanks." He shook his head. "But I have somewhere I gotta be."

"Whatever," she muttered, pulling another cigarette out of her pack as she looked away from him. He walked away without another word, moving off the block and around the corner, the path now shrouded in darkness from broken streetlights. He knew she'd be coming down any minute.

Moving into the shadows again, he reached into his jacket and pulled out the tool he planned to use, a double-barrel shotgun that had been sawed off into a handgun.

He crouched to one knee, waiting for the sound of her shoes to click-clack on the sidewalk as he remained silent. The sounds started up. He knew she was coming his way.

He gripped the handle tightly and the barrels with his free hand, intent on utilizing it to its maximum capacity.

She walked down to the corner, her back turned to him as he moved closer and rose to his feet, holding the weapon up to the back of her head. He let out a yelp, earning her attention, her head turning around quickly to see what the origin of the noise was.

He pulled the triggers and emptied both barrels inches from her face, completely splattering her head all over the street; the explosion of the gunshot echoed. Acting quickly, he dropped to his knees and reached into his other inner coat pocket, pulling out the hunting knife that had been sharpened for the occasion.

Henry realized this was as good a time as any, raising himself over the woman's body, intent on enjoying all she had to offer. Unzipping himself, he used the blade to cut away her lower garment and pushed himself inside of her hole. It was still warm, as was her entire body; her face was not much to look at, though.

He moved atop her body, laying the side of his face against her still breasts. The lack of her chest moving up and down was slightly disconcerting. Yet, it was just enough for him; she was still tight within.

He slammed quicker and harder, intent on finishing within her body, knowing that soon the bugs and rats would be out for dinner.

Whimpering pathetically, Henry reached his point and spilled himself inside the body. He had to get to work. He had to get to the point of this activity. It was time to get to the even better reason for taking the woman down.

Reaching down, he proceeded to cut through the dead woman's heels, hacking them away from her long, blood-splashed legs and returning the knife to his jacket pocket.

Her entire body was covered in blood from the effect of her head exploding. Her legs were bloody where her feet had been removed. Her thin body practically broke upon hitting the cold ground so hard. It was no way for anyone to die, but he wanted what he wanted, and he had to get it, one way or another.

Taking a trash bag from his outer pocket, he opened it and stuffed the severed feet adorned with the red stilettos into the bag, tying the top in a quick knot.

Getting back up, he turned away from the scene and left the area, moving back toward the destination of his car. He was satisfied with what he'd just done. It was the best feeling. He knew those feet and shoes would be excellent additions to his collection. He felt his cock twitch as the urge to relieve himself on the stilettos was growing heavier by the moment.

No, he thought to himself.

He would wait until he got home.

Just a walk to the car and then a short drive after that, and he was free to partake in the spoils of his little hunt. The sky was overcast with clouds, the moon was covered, and the fog was growing thicker. He was going to have a long walk ahead, but that was no issue for him; he got what he desired most of all.

He couldn't explain it.

It was just something he had a strong urge for.

The bag held tightly in his hand, he licked his lips and again felt the zit on his upper lip, goddamnit. It was going to be a pain in the ass to remove it or wait till it removed itself, just like everything else.

Making his way down sidewalks toward the parking lot after walking what seemed like forever, he saw cars driving by and people randomly moving about, back to the populated area of the downtown city limits. It was nice to see people again. Especially people who were in the hustle and bustle of trying to get home before last call at the bar.

Walking through the parking lot, he finally reached his car and hit the button to unlock the doors, opening the driver's side to unlock the trunk.

Heading to the back of the car, he reached down to raise the trunk and lifted the bag to set it inside the trunk space before opening it quickly to get a sneak peek at his prizes. He licked his lips, releasing a soft moan, the glare of the orange trunk light on the red leather of the stilettos forcing him to reveal his admiration. However, he had to get out before the toll time ended, and he'd have to pay more, so he closed the trunk.

Getting into the driver's seat, he closed the door and wiped his face, looking down to realize he had blood splatter on his right side. It must have happened when the shotgun blew the woman's head off. *Damn*, he sighed while wiping the blood off his face as best he could. It must have been a bigger blast than he'd thought.

Sticking the key in the ignition, he turned the engine over, and the car started up, the warm air of the heater immediately blowing in his face. He'd head home and prepare to enjoy the goods he'd taken, like a greedy kid outside of a candy store. He got his treats.

Now, he just needed to appreciate them properly.

CHAPTER THREE

Stephanie West slowly rubbed her eyes as she woke with a slight headache. Turning her head, she looked at her alarm clock and saw that it was a quarter after six in the morning—a whole thirty minutes before the clock was going to go off and wake her in preparation for the new day.

She turned back to look up at the dark ceiling before reaching over to the pack of cigs on the bedside table and the accompanying lighter, popping one in her mouth before lighting it up. Taking a drag of tobacco that filled her lungs and exhaled with a hard cough, she sighed. Life was already a joke for her, but now she was beating the alarm clock and losing precious sleep.

Burnout was a real thing, and she had been burning for far too long, regardless of the days when she felt like she was actually doing some good in the world.

Taking a deeper drag and holding the smoke in her lungs as she considered the pros and cons of calling in to work, she rolled her eyes before exhaling the smoke. Sitting up on the bed, she set the cigarette in the ashtray near the alarm clock and turned on the lamp, illuminating the room. Sitting against the wall with her pillow under her lower back, she looked around the tiny bedroom of her apartment as her eyes analyzed everything that covered the walls and shelves.

The walls were covered in awards she had been given over the last ten years as a member of the city's police force. Of course, they meant little to nothing in the grand scheme of things, but at the time, she was quite proud to receive each and every one of them. If she had ever had a girlfriend, she knew they would probably also appreciate the awards.

Unfortunately, that was not in the cards for her, and she got to look forward to another year spent living alone in her apartment. It was almost impossible to have a functioning long-time relationship with anyone when you spent every waking hour solving cases in a city that never slept.

Well, the people slept, but crime never did.

Taking the cigarette from the ashtray, Stephanie placed it back between her lips before taking a long drag and exhaling as she decided to forgo calling in. No, she would go to work and do her job, just like every other day. Taking one last drag from the cigarette, she smashed it out in the ashtray before getting out of bed and heading toward the kitchen to beat the timer on the coffee maker.

Pressing the button on the coffee maker, she leaned against the counter as she listened to the machine start to percolate and coughed slightly again. *Fucking cigs.* She knew she had to give up the little cancer sticks before they started to do lasting damage to her lungs. She was nearing her late thirties and didn't want to face a breathless future hooked up to an oxygen tank.

Reaching into the cabinet after pulling open the door, Stephanie grabbed her favorite mango colored mug and set it beside the coffee machine as the dark brown liquid started to fill the pot. She was ready to get caffeinated and start the day off like every other, especially since she knew she would be bombarded with a full caseload upon entering the office.

Once the machine finished percolating and revealed itself to be complete, she gripped the handle of the pot before pouring the bitter liquid into the mug. Grabbing the small ceramic container marked **Sugar**, Stephanie removed the lid and scooped out three small spoonfuls of the soft white granules to add to the steaming cup of brew, stirring the sweet into the bitter for an overpowering jet-fuel.

Taking the mug in hand, Stephanie sauntered into the living room before sitting on the sofa and switching on the small television to check the local happenings. The news was never good and was most likely bullshit, but it was entertaining enough while she sipped her morning coffee.

Routines were something Stephanie found herself attached to. She was always set in her ways, and when she couldn't follow a routine to the max, she felt herself quickly overcome with anxiety. She had been this way ever since she was a child, and no matter how much she tried to explain to those around her, it never seemed to matter to anyone but her. Thankfully, her aunt had managed to get her into therapy sessions, and while it never cured her of her needs, it did help her find a way to channel her anxiety into less-destructive displays.

Sipping the coffee despite its heat, the woman watched the news reporters drone on about local happenings in the city. It was always the same story. Crime was a never-ending plague that seemed to keep everyone down and prevent the world from actually progressing. Then again, it also kept her in business with solving the intricacies and paid for her relatively cheap lifestyle, so there was that.

She took another sip as she flipped the channel on the television to another boring sitcom about some inane bullshit and watched without cracking a smile as she finished her cup of coffee.

After finishing up, she finally lifted herself off the sofa and headed toward the bedroom as it had come time to get ready for the work day. Stephanie opened her closet door and selected her beige pantsuit that always felt comfortable on her skin.

She had a certain thing about the feel and texture of certain materials, but like with most things, she had learned to deal with the issues that created. Pulling off her pink long shirt, Stephanie turned to the mirror and took a second to admire her figure.

She was pleased with the way that she looked, especially after spending every other week in the gym when she got off work. Her body was firm, her legs were long and lean, her abs were tight, and she had a modest-sized bust. Best of all, she had a round and firm ass that really didn't have any flaws. She might not have been a model or a cover girl, but she was proud of her appearance regardless.

Dressing in her pantsuit, Stephanie pulled her badge up from the bedside table and clipped it onto her belt before slipping on her shoes. They were soft and stretchy, easy to walk in, and everything that shoes should be when one was constantly on the go.

She had a habit of making sure everything was perfect down to the last detail. It wasn't very popular with the people she worked with or interacted with, but Stephanie was less interested in social activities than she was in ensuring that everything was correct. It was a casualty of the therapy sessions; some things just never changed.

Making sure that she had everything she needed, the detective grabbed her keys from the bedside table and slid them into her coat pocket before turning off the lamp. She'd have one more cup of coffee and then head out to the office, all while wishing she had called out. It wasn't like she would be facing anything new or unheard of, especially since life had a way of ensuring she didn't get those types of cases.

Grabbing her bag, Stephanie exited her apartment and locked the door behind her, fighting the urge to go back inside without a care in the world.

Chapter Four

Slowly, the scalpel pulled down the soft, blue-tinted flesh and carved open the space to reveal the spine from within the tiny corpse. Heat from the lamp overhead forced sweat to run down Doctor Black's forehead as he focused intently on scraping the area clear.

It was one of the icky parts of this project, but it had to be done with excellent precision. The flesh came off without resistance. It was simple and easy, but this was normal with rotting epidermis. Sniffing behind the face mask, Black cleared his throat in a wet gurgle and proceeded to dig the blade of the scalpel deeper into the tiny spinal cord of the corpse, procuring the samples he needed for the mixture.

Stem cells were a key component for the concoction that was brewing away on the table beside him. The creamy substance that oozed out of broken infant spinal cords would be the special biological ingredient that would help fix any flaws that he had overlooked. The crackle of the spine being cut out of the corpse filled his ears, and he couldn't help but chuckle at the way he must have looked. Needless to say, he had quite a few spines to go before he had enough material, but this was all part of the plan.

It wasn't going to be easy, but few things in life ever were.

Using a pair of tweezers, Black lifted the carved piece of spine from the corpse and placed it in the center of a clear plastic container before sealing the lid. Raising, he wiped the sweat from his forehead and turned in his stool to look at the next fetal corpse lying on the table beside him. The endeavor was looking up as he realized he'd nearly finished one whole container and was soon to be onto the next one.

Getting up from the stool, Black walked over to the mixture that was bubbling slowly on the table filled with chemicals. He ran his fingertip down the list of notes he'd jotted and tapped on the final three ingredients he'd need:

Bull Shark DNA

Human Stem Cells

Biological fetal materials

Smiling behind the face mask, he realized he had all three of the components on hand, and once he squeezed the cream from the spines, he'd be able to mark stem cells off the list.

Walking over to the third container, Black used the scalpel to pop open the lid and peered down to take a look at what was within: fetal remains floating in thick plastic bags of amnion and nutritious afterbirth goo. The smell was certainly something to be desired, but at this point, Black couldn't care less about such trivial misfortunes.

Raising one of the bags from within, he chuckled as he watched the chunks of fetus bobbing up and down in the thick pink liquid before shaking his head. To think that abortion clinics just threw this shit out with yesterday's lunch was a crime against humanity.

The remains could be used for much bigger purposes. He'd show them all the true use of aborted pregnancy release. These bags had uses for almost anything. He'd heard a story a while back about a massacre that took place in an old abortion clinic, and one of the victims had been forced to choke to death on a bag of aborted remains.

Waste of good material as far as he was concerned.

Cracking open the bag, Black reached into his gloved hand within the bag and pulled up a handful of chunks as the fluids ran down his hand to the floor below. He smiled widely as he looked it over, speaking softly. "Don't worry, little one, your sacrifice is going to pave the way to a much greater future, I promise you that."

Dropping the chunks unceremoniously back into the bag, Black took the bag in hand and set it on the table near the concoction in the beaker. Taking a glass syringe with a long needle attached, the scientist opened the bag wider and dipped the needle into the viscous fluid before slowly pulling the plunger back to collect a load in the space of the syringe.

After filling it, Black flicked the needle with his middle finger and held it over the beaker of mixed chemicals as he pressed the plunger back down. The afterbirth fluids slowly exited through the needle into the bubbling liquids within. He watched with eager intent as the color of the formula turned a bright red within the beaker.

Setting the syringe aside, Black sealed the plastic bag of fetal remains and walked back to the makeshift operating table.

Pulling the mask down to rest on his neck, the scientist reached down to grab another corpse and prepare it for surgery. The new corpse was later-term and almost completely formed, despite a small defect on the right foot. Shaking his head, he gripped the scalpel and placed the corpse on its front before sitting back on the stool. The stem cells were what he was after, not the corpse and certainly not anything else it could provide. He was ensuring a future for others and that negated all the unforgivable shit he was currently working on; he wasn't some Nazi fuck that enjoyed this kind of activity; he simply wanted to create something that would bring relief to the world.

Especially if it meant that it would bring some pride to his name and profession. One too many times had he been laughed out of university and the facility for "crackpot theories." No, not this time; he would prove how wrong everyone was in judging him as a madman. He was not going to forgo his hopes and dreams, even if it meant he had to get his hands dirty and Sully any chance he had in getting into heaven.

Fuck that.

It was then that Black looked over to one of the windows he hadn't boarded up and realized the sun was starting to shine from outside. Damn, he'd worked through the night. He'd have to take a nap soon or face the chance of screwing up his work. Sighing, Black shook his head to clear his mind and turned back to the work at hand. One more small surgery would get him ahead of schedule.

Just one more.

Taking the scalpel in hand, he began slicing through the upper portion of the neck and scraping away the flesh to reveal the spine of the corpse. The way that the flesh peeled right off was almost gut-wrenching, but at the same time, he was glad that he didn't have to fight with the epidermis of a fetal corpse. There were a lot worse things in life.

Cracking through the spine as he had done previously, Black smirked before realizing he hadn't placed the mask back on his face. Groaning, he reached down to pull it back in place and set the scalpel down before using the tweezers to pull the spine from the corpse.

Lifting the bit of material to view it in the light, he couldn't help but marvel at it. If he was a freak, he'd probably turn the leftover spines into some form of macabre jewelry for the delinquent edgelords to wear. Some people get off to that kind of sick shit, but no, they'd go in a waste bin after being squeezed dry for the nutritious cells within.

He wasn't about to feed anyone's fucked up desires. Not when there was a fortune to be made in crafting the perfect formula for infant intelligence.

Principles mattered, he thought to himself before dumping the rest of the corpse into the waste bucket next to the makeshift operating table.

CHAPTER FIVE

Pulling into his driveway as the morning sun lit up the middle-class neighborhood, Henry killed the engine and breathed slowly, conserving his strength as he set out to follow through with his ritual.

Popping the trunk and getting out of his car, he walked around back to open the trunk and grab the bag after tying it shut again. Closing the trunk, he walked up to the front door of his house and used his key to unlock it, walking into the house as he did. He turned and shut the door, locking it back before turning around. Immediately, he noticed the television on with the volume low and his wife sitting in one of the rocking chairs, a blanket covering her legs as a soft snore exited her mouth.

Smiling, he moved with ease through the living room, past the kitchen, and toward the door of the garage.

It was a spacious garage that he'd long ago customized into his man-cave. Sally, his wife, knew he liked to be alone for long periods and didn't question it, knowing better than to interfere with his quirks. He wasn't a violent or abusive man, but he could be passive-aggressive in a way that could lead to arguments nobody had time for. Sally had learned to appreciate the time away when he needed to be isolated.

It was all part of their successful marriage.

Their friends all talked about how great Henry and Sally were as a couple, and how their kids were some of the most well-mannered they'd ever seen. It was a point of pride for Henry. He liked being admired by people, especially people he knew somewhat well and had shared a beer with, a time or two.

Entering the garage with his special set of keys, Henry turned on the lights and illuminated the area, cutting through the darkness to reveal everything about it he loved.

A desk sat off to the side, along with his leather rolling chair, and the walls had pictures he'd taped up, displaying various things that interested him. Across from the desk was a converted closet space holding his most beloved treasures. Walking to the desk, Henry opened the bag and pulled the bloodied feet and stilettos out to sit on the desk.

Looking around after tossing the bag in the trash, he grabbed a roll of paper towels and a spray bottle of water, taking a seat in the leather chair to focus on cleaning it all up. Spraying water on the feet, he set out to remove all of the blood from the skin and around the jagged tops of the heels.

The toenails were perfectly manicured, even bearing a shade of ruby nail polish, shining in the overhead lamp of the garage.

He caressed the feet, feeling himself growing more and more turned on by them; the way the toes were shaped was interesting to him. Rarely had he seen such a set of toes, the second toe nearly longer than the big toe, unusual but exotic. Setting the foot aside, he cleaned the next one, and that's when he spotted it, a small golden ring around the second toe of the right foot. The woman had toe jewelry, so fucking hot, it was incredible.

After he finished cleaning the feet, he cleaned up the shoes while taking delicate care to remove any and all flecks of blood from the red leather. The spiked heels were a nice touch. The way the shoes looked, the way they stood up when placed on a desk or a chair, or the floor, was unbelievably erotic in his mind.

Taking off his shoes and socks, Henry set the stilettos in front of him to slide his feet into. Thankfully, he always had smaller feet and they would fit, albeit a bit tightly inside the stilettos themselves. Sitting back in the chair, Henry unzipped his trousers to pull out his tool and felt his toes wiggling inside the red high-heels. They were so beautiful and sensual, he moved his hand along the length of his pole.

He was hot, now.

It was going to be a good rub.

Raising his right leg and admiring the shoe on his foot, he turned his foot side to side, jerking as he looked at the view of the shoe. It was hot. She had been hot. Sliding his left foot out of the shoe, he moved it back up to the desk and removed his hand from his cock, using it to hold the shoe still as he placed one of the cleaved feet into the shoe.

After it was done, he returned to stroking, looking at the foot in the shoe. The imagery was explosively delicious. The firm flesh of the white food stationed in the upright support of the crimson stiletto stood for his view, intent on staying for his pleasure. *Fuck!* He began to sweat as he stroked himself faster and quicker.

It was getting close. He could feel himself getting close. The passion burned inside of him. The way the woman had been walking, sauntering, sashaying, putting her feet to work while using the heels was so breathtaking. He couldn't stop himself.

He had to taste the toes.

Reaching over to take the right foot in his grasp, he moved it to his mouth, licking and sucking the toes as he jerked himself.

It was so fucking hot.

Moving his mouth over the big toe, he sucked it and licked the tip within his mouth, stroking quicker as he moved his hand in a back and forth motion. The taste of the soft flesh on his tongue, the feel of the stiletto on his foot, and the sight of the other foot in a stiletto teasing him on the desk proved too much.

Henry reached his climax while keeping the toes in his mouth and wiggling the foot around with his hand. It was heavenly.

This was paradise.

It was the best feeling, the pleasure overwhelming and the ecstasy invigorating; he loved every bit of it. Finally, he removed his hand from the withering tool in his pants and pulled the toes from his mouth, setting the foot back down on the desk. Pulling off the shoe from his foot, he rose slowly, carrying the scarlet stilettos into the closet space and placed them in a near-perfect position amongst the others.

There were many high heels in the collection.

Hundreds.

Perhaps even thousands.

It was the most beautiful thing he had ever seen. So many high-heels, low pumps, and platform heels. They were his crown jewels. He loved them more than he loved anything, except Sally, whom he had asked to wear them to bed on nights he felt like plying her with some of the physical charm she'd fallen for years prior.

He'd been at this gig for years, and the city provided plenty of victims for his collection. Police were a joke. He'd been worried in the beginning, but rarely did he ever have any trouble from the cops. The city had more criminals than cops, the perfect place for a serial killer to ply his trade and reap the rewards.

Zipping up his pants, Henry took a long look at the shoes and turned off the light in the closet, turning to face the next task at hand.

He had to save his feet. They were fun, and he lusted after them. They modeled his shoes and gave him the aid when he needed to fleece himself for being so bad.

Reaching into the cabinet under the counter against the wall near the closet, Henry pulled out the bucket of epoxy resin and raised it, setting the bucket on the counter. Cracking open the lid, he walked over to grab the feet and placed them in an empty container. He'd cast them into molds that would keep for many years to come.

Suddenly, it hit him.

The toe ring.

It looked nice, but he knew it wouldn't work with the resin. Raising the right foot to his mouth, he sucked the toes between his lips and slowly removed the ring with his teeth, taking care not to graze the skin of the toe along the way. Spitting the ring onto the counter, he placed the foot back in the container and poured the resin into it, intent on filling it up.

After finishing this, Henry killed the light and headed for the door, ready to sleep the day away before going on the prowl again. He was tired but satiated.

It had been a good day's work.

Chapter Six

Sitting at her desk in the small office, Stephanie busied herself with filling out a report on the case she'd been pursuing the last few weeks. Thankfully, everything had been taken care of, and she was finished, aside from a few bits of paperwork that needed to be filed.

Her fingers swiftly typed on the keyboard while her glasses rested firmly on the bridge of her nose. She enjoyed typing. If she ever got the chance, she'd even consider writing a book about one of her cases in a true crime fiction setting. Unfortunately, it seemed like she was never going to get that chance, especially whenever there was a nonstop pile of case folders being plopped on her desk every so often.

As if on cue, another officer, Sgt. Collins entered her office holding a folder in his hands. Turning to look at him, Stephanie sighed, "What's this one about?"

"I don't know," the older man smirked, "Maybe you should open it and find out?"

Stephanie glared at Collins. He was balding, wore a thick pair of horn-rimmed glasses over his beady eyes, and his white dress shirt was stained from a particularly messy sandwich he'd consumed for breakfast.

Charming.

Nodding, Stephanie turned to face the desk and took the folder from his hands to lay before her on the surface. The older officer crossed his arms and said, "Good job with the Henderson case. I bet the chief is just dying to give you another plaque."

"Is that jealousy I'm hearing in your tone?" Stephanie inquired, not bothering to look up from the open folder. Collins simply sneered. "You're the big detective, why don't you figure it out?"

Looking up from barely glancing at the words, she stared at Collins. "So it *is* jealousy, or something close to that effect?"

"I'm not *jealous*," Collins scoffed, "I'm just saying you make the rest of us look like amateurs when you get on the ball. I'm sure your family must be really proud of your ability to be some kind of television super-sleuth."

"My family's dead," Stephanie replied coldly before finishing with a dismissive tone, "Thank you for the case folder."

Collins uncrossed his arms and nodded in annoyance before exiting the office without another word. Unwilling to give any more attention to the jealous whining of a coworker, Stephanie lowered her gaze to the open report and quickly read through the lines of information.

A murder took place in one of the red light districts that filled the city. The victim had been a streetwalker, killed execution style with a high-powered shotgun, and the feet had been removed with a blade. The murder seemed professional, but the removal of the extremities had the distinct look of one not trained in surgical practice.

The case had all the details of several others that had been taking place throughout the city in the last four years. Stephanie had heard other detectives talking about it, but she'd never been given the chance to take part in the investigation herself. She hadn't questioned it, especially since the department had a massive haul of cases being handed to her and the subliminal amount of sexism that took place regularly regarding female detectives.

However, now she was being given the chance to take part in the investigation, and it would prove to be a challenge to her skills. Still, she couldn't help but question why she was suddenly being given the opportunity to assist with the case of the Foot Carver.

Shaking her head, she forced herself to study the case more and put to rest the urge to question a good thing. The Henderson case had been simple enough. It was a plot to pull off a jewelry store insurance scam. Too bad the owner had defaulted on his insurance payments before hiring an arsonist to firebomb his building.

No, this time Stephanie had real stakes.

The Foot Carver had been killing, mutilating, and leaving bodies all over the city for years. They were always women. She'd seen the news reports on television during her morning coffee. The department had done a monumentally piss-poor job of investigating the crimes as they came along. She wanted to blame the backlog of cases, but that wasn't going to be enough.

The department was just damn lazy in her opinion. The city was replete with nonstop violent acts. Half of the department was on the take, and the other half simply didn't care about anything that went on that they couldn't control or stop in a short amount of time. Unfortunately, it seemed that that had been the way of the land since long before she had joined the force. The men in the department always seemed to get the hardcore cases that left people with nightmares, and the women in the department got the *less* interesting bits that were left over.

She'd spent ten years working cases and putting together puzzle after puzzle, but they always felt like empty victories. Now lives were at stake, and she had been given the ticket to find clues that the rest of the incompetent men in the department couldn't be bothered to properly locate or report.

Stephanie didn't have much faith in the ability of men to do much of anything beyond the bare minimum that they could provide. She wasn't sexist toward the male gender; she just knew that women were a bit more detail-oriented.

Looking through the paperwork in the folder, Stephanie took a mental note of everything she read, hoping to discover some form of key element that had so far been unnoticed. She couldn't help the overwhelming feeling of anxiety crawling up on her as she scanned every word and sentence. Perhaps she was setting herself up for failure already by being too excited about the case. Perhaps this was Collins trying to fuck with her. He had been jealous of her success rate, and this would be the perfect opportunity for her to fail.

No.

She had to disregard the faulty emotions in her brain. Shaking her head, Stephanie got up from the desk and turned to face the window, looking out at the city. She watched the cars driving to and from their destinations, and stared into the abyss of the busy streets while counting her breaths. She had to get it under control.

She had to keep from having a meltdown.

This was the practice that kept her focused and calm. She crossed her arms to hold herself tightly and rocked back and forth slowly. Everything would be okay, she told herself, everything would be fine.

After all, she had been working for so long, and things always came up with a satisfying conclusion. It wasn't likely that Collins would purposefully try to fuck her up. He was a prick, but he wasn't evil like the Foot Carver, who was out to fill some sick need.

The need must have been particularly deep for them. Why did they hack off the feet? Perhaps for trophies? It could have been a compulsion. Stephanie was knowledgeable about compulsions and the need to follow them. Then again, it could be something connected to the feet themselves.

It would make sense, especially if the killer had some form of connection or deep-rooted interest in the feet.

Slowly coming to a halt in rocking herself, Stephanie took a deep breath and turned back to the folder on the desk. She knew that it was not uncommon for people to feel anxious or work themselves into a state of biting worry, but she hated it whenever it happened at work. It was another reason why she didn't socialize with anyone, coworkers, or civilians. Even if Collins had been working to uproot her routine, she would have to pretend that it wasn't bothering her as much as it was. After all, this was a potentially bad theory regarding the case. However, it was a theory worth pursuing.

Sitting at her desk, she proceeded to read through the file again and realized the shoes had not been found at the scene of the crime. She rapped her fingertips on the desk. It was a small detail, but it was something that may have been connected to the other cases regarding the Foot Carver. She swallowed as she considered her next move.

It was time to visit the file office and find every case she could that was tied to the killer, directly or indirectly. One thing was certain for her at that moment.

This was going to be an all-day marathon of search and discovery.

Chapter Seven

Henry woke in bed and stretched out, yawning as he did practically every day after waking.

Getting up, Henry's first stop was to hit the toilet, and after finishing up the stream, he walked into the kitchen. Sally was slaving away over the stove, sipping coffee and dressed in her nightgown affixed with a white and pink apron. He smiled as he looked at her from behind. She had a cute ass, as always, especially when her long slender legs were supported by the pair of black high-heels he'd given her. She was wearing them.

She knew he liked heels.

He spoke to her as he came up behind her, wrapping his arm around her stomach, "Morning."

"Good morning, Mister All-Nighter," she replied, smiling as she felt him place a few kisses down the back of her neck. He was an affectionate man. It was why she'd fallen for him in the first place. Her family hated him, but alas, it just pushed her into his arms even more. He was a soft-spoken type who treated her like a queen.

It was perfect.

She loved him to death.

At the table sat their son, Richard, and their daughter, Liz, both too busy eating their breakfast to see their parents' overblown affection. Henry turned to them and smiled, "Morning, kids. Sleep well?"

"Yeah," Liz replied, looking up to smile, her legs rocking back and forth under the table while Richard shrugged, looking down at his pancakes. Henry poured a cup of coffee, sitting at the head of the table, and took a heavy sigh; it was the perfect life. This was everything he had hoped for, even at a young age; it was beautiful.

Sally set a plate of eggs, sausage, and pancakes in front of him, tossing her towelette over her shoulder and said, "Enjoy."

Henry looked up at her, smiled brightly, and began to consume the hearty breakfast. It was one of Sally's specialties. She'd learned good cooking from her mother years ago, yet she put her own spin on it and made it better than ever, definitely something to wake up to every day. Henry ate quickly, intent on getting dressed and looking for a potential victim to add to his collection.

Some men were businessmen, some men were blue-collar, and some were self-starters; Henry was a hunter.

Eating the last bite consisting of egg, sausage, and syrup, Henry got up from the table and kissed Sally's cheek. "I gotta get dressed and make a run into the city. I shouldn't be gone long."

"Okay, if I give you a list, can you pick up some things for dinner tonight?"

"Certainly."

"Okay, sweetheart," she smiled, watching him retreat to the bedroom. She knew he had a business. She didn't know what he did, other than his statement that he once made that he traded in personal goods, but it put food on the table and kept the roof over their heads, in addition to her own job as a bank secretary. The income was good enough.

She didn't need to be rich.

She just needed to be stable.

Henry slipped into his slacks, put on one of his bowling shirts from back when he used to bowl competitively, and slid on his trust overcoat. It was worn, but it was also comfortable, and he wasn't the type to throw anything away because it had gotten a bit of age. He had a lot of miles on the coat.

And it was good for many more.

He exited the bedroom to get into the garage and shut the door behind him, locking it up, then walked over to the counter where the feet were sitting, cast perfectly and shining in the light of the garage, they looked almost plastic. However, he knew better and grabbed his suitcase, opening it up to settle his feet within it.

Snapping it closed, he turned to exit the garage, but stopped for a brief moment. They were calling him. The urge was calling him again. He felt himself getting hard as he felt the urge to peruse the shoes hit him. Setting down the suitcase, he walked across to the closet and turned on the light within, looking down at all of the shoes.

Each pair had a story.

Some were rescues, some were bought, and most were taken.

The best were the ones that he'd earned from his hunts.

Reaching down, Henry picked up a pair of velvet purple pumps he had taken off of a college girl that he had followed to an empty parking garage weeks earlier and ripped open her neck. Her body had bled out, her mouth twitching as she attempted to cry for help, alive while he cleaved her feet from her body. The pumps were so perfect.

Reaching down, he unzipped his pants and pulled out his tool, using both hands to hold the tops of the pumps while mashing his rigid member with the bottom and tip of the front of the shoes. He was teasing himself. It was hot. He could picture a pair of feet from a woman within the shoes, giving him a footjob while she talked down to him.

He loved when women treated him like shit.

Sally never did; she worshiped him, and he hated it.

He could remember the way his mother had belittled him, the way she tormented him, and forced him to throw away the heels he'd found at a landfill. He'd just play there occasionally, acting out magical fantasies and fighting dragons in his mind, until he spotted the heels. They were the most incredible things he had ever seen, and he brought them home, wearing them despite their larger size.

Oh, he felt himself getting toward the last round.

His mother, angry at his perceived show of femininity, had forced him to toss them out. Yet, he rebelled and kept them, stashing them away to wear late at night as he walked in his bedroom. She had found them. She burned them. She took away his heels, and it burned him badly, the way she had belittled him in front of his older brothers and his father.

Yet he liked it.

They looked down at him. The intense hate he felt fueled his fire and he knew one day he'd get more heels, yet the bitching was something he had to fantasize about, which he did over and over again. Being nothing more than a man beaten down verbally by a woman while she used her shoe to get him off rather than actually using effort, knowing it was below her and that he was as well. He wanted it so much.

He moaned as he came, spilling his warm white all over the purple velvet of the pumps, and he shivered as the last bit came out in spurts, his body releasing again.

Shaking his head to clear his mind, Henry swallowed and set the shoes down in the closet, jiggling the last out of his pole. Zipping himself up, he turned to exit the garage and shut off the light.

Time to prepare for the hunt..

Chapter Eight

The irritating buzz of an alarm clock brought Dr. Black out of his slumber, forcing him to swing open his eyelids and look around the dimly-lit warehouse, smiling as he stretched out his arm to grab the clock and slam his other hand onto the top of it, silencing the ringing bells that were mounted to the top.

"That's better," he mumbled before dropping it back to the floor and slowly throwing his legs over the side of the hammock he'd been sleeping in. Rubbing his eyes to push the sleep out of them, he cleared his throat and looked across the room to his workspace.

Perfect.

He was ready to get back to work and add the next ingredient to his concoction. It was going to be a fun afternoon.

Getting up from the hammock, Black twisted from side-to-side before walking toward the large table filled with beakers galore, reaching down to scratch his ass as he sauntered up to remove the cover of the glass beaker containing his formula. Cracking his knuckles, he looked down the list and tapped his fingertip on the next ingredient to add.

Shark DNA.

Thankfully, he'd kept the material in the freezer, ensuring that the valuable component remained fresh in its bag. Turning toward the freezer that was positioned against the wall, Black walked to the large white laydown container and took hold of the lid, lifting it off its magnetic anchor to feel the frigid air rising from within. He scanned the interior before his eyes landed directly on the plastic bag of opaque genetic material. Reaching in and taking hold, Black pulled the bag out before closing the lid while walking back to the table.

As he returned, the scientist proceeded to pull open the bag of thick liquid and took a whiff of the odor that left him with a fishy scent in his nostrils. Shivering slightly from the remnants of cold air that lingered on his skin, Black proceeded to grasp a glass syringe that he hadn't used yet and forced the needle into the thickened material, briefly contemplating just how much to pull out for the addition to his formula.

He did not want the shark DNA to overwhelm the other chemicals and ingredients of the serum, but he also knew that the DNA was the key ingredient in terms of providing advanced intelligence for the future patients. Finally, after weighing the amounts in his mind, Black withdrew twenty cubic centimeters of the material before lifting the syringe from the bag and placing it on the table.

Grabbing the small box of matches, the doctor pulled one of the sticks from within and struck the red phosphorus to procure a small flame that he used to ignite the burner underneath the beaker of formula. Tapping his fingers on the surface of the table, he proceeded to ignore the hunger pains from within his stomach while slowly watching the liquid begin to simmer and bubble within the glass container. He knew he had to eat at some point today, but for now, he was going to focus on getting the project finished and setting it up for the test subjects.

It was then that he realized he may have forgotten the most important part of this entire setup. He didn't have any test subjects to practice the experiment on. Taking a heavy sigh, Black hurriedly walked toward the other table that had less clutter on the surface and gripped the receiver of the phone before dialing the two men he'd paid to pick up the shark DNA from the shipping dock. Holding it up to his ear and waiting patiently as it rang, he was slowly feeling anxiety building up in his chest as he realized the blunder of an oversight that he had made.

Finally, a voice answered on the other end, "Hello?"

"Rory, it's Doctor Black. I need you and your brother to pick up another component of my experiment."

"Another trip to the docks?"

"No," Black replied, contemplating how to explain it before shaking his head, "This pick up will require a bit of legwork, but I promise I'll pay triple what I did before."

"Triple? Damn, I assume you'll want it by tonight?"

"Yes, however, I need to explain to you both in private what I need. Can the two of you get over here within the next hour or so?"

"Yeah," the voice replied while making a soft noise that one makes when stretching, "We'll head that way."

"Thank you," Black replied before hanging up the receiver on the base and breathing a heavy sigh of relief. Thank God there were still reliable people in the world. True, money was a huge instrument in retaining the reliability of people and their abilities, but it was an instrument that Black knew how to play almost professionally. Thankfully, his family had left him a rather large fortune, and it not only paid for his college studies but also managed to help fund every little part of the experiment that he was sinking countless days into. It wasn't all gone, but it definitely needed a bit of an infusion to rebuild what had been spent.

Doctor Black knew that the experiment would pay off once he perfected and utilized it for the population of the world; therefore, it made all of his expenditures worthwhile. And since he didn't have any kids of his own to pass the fortune along to, it was probably best that he used it for the betterment of mankind rather than it being left to the city for whatever vile purpose they would create.

Shaking his head, the scientist felt the pain of hunger rumbling within his stomach again and knew that he needed to fill the empty hole before plotting the next move for his formula. Pulling the receiver off the base again, he proceeded to dial in the number to the local pizza shop and waited for them to answer. A response came after four rings, "Major's Pizza, how can I help you?"

"Yeah, I need a pie with everything on it, except anchovies and peppers."

"O-kay, anything else?"

"I'll take a soda, too."

"Will that be for pickup or delivery?"

"Delivery."

"Where to?"

"Twenty-Fifth and Chambers, building 3; I'll meet the driver outside."

"O-kay, we'll get it ready and sent it out. Thank you for ordering Major's Pizza."

"Hey, thank you," Black replied before hanging up the phone and nodding. It was definitely going to be a good day. Looking over to see the formula bubbling in its container, he quickly moved back to it and turned off the flame of the burner, watching with intent as the bubbling froth died down while steam rose from the light red liquid within.

He smiled at the formula, whispering, "My pride and joy, my dream, you're going to make me a very wealthy man."

Writing down his notes on the sketchpad that was near the burner, Black cleared his throat and snapped his fingers as he grabbed the syringe in his right hand to angle it into the beaker. Slowly, he pressed the plunger down with his thumb to add the shark DNA to the mixture. Seconds passed as the syringe emptied into the formula. He could feel his breathing getting stronger.

Black smiled and pulled the needle from inside the beaker, setting the syringe down; the addition was complete. He scribbled in his pad and turned to the next ingredient before snagging a pair of white rubber gloves. It was time to break down and add the stem cells.

He'd harvested them from the aborted fetuses, and before falling asleep, he'd harvested them from the body of the driver. The volume was abundant, and there was little chance he'd need to procure anymore. No, he was set for quite some time.

It was good to have a quantity.

Chapter Nine

Driving into the city, Henry looked around to see the pedestrians dotting the sidewalks, all moving to and from their places of work. Everyone was in a hurry. It was almost a ritual for people to be so rushed.

Driving to the store to do some shopping for Sally, Henry considered his options; a stripper might have what he was looking for. However, that was a mixed bag; chances were that she might have implants, and the breasts would be useless if he cut them off with the implants being punctured. Scratching that plan, he made a mental note, pulling into the parking lot of the store and turning off the car.

Shopping was not something Henry enjoyed, but he knew that anything he got would be a masterpiece once Sally got her hands on it and whipped up dinner.

Moving down the aisles of the store, Henry tossed a few items in his cart and went on with the thought in his head, where to secure the goods. He needed to find someone who was of the right age, who was firm and fit, someone who had a pair of heels that worked in her favor. But alas, it wasn't like someone of that caliber was gonna show up out of the blue.

Suddenly, he spotted someone close enough.

A worker.

It was one of the store employees, Emily, a buxom woman with a round face and long curly hair, dressed in a flowing skirt and wearing a pair of black high heels on her thin feet. The heels gave her a bit of height, and her shirt definitely was on the verge of popping a button from the intensity of her breasts. She was excellent.

A perfect target.

She would be a better Target than almost any of the women he had hunted over the last year. It was as if he had been struck by a freaking lightning bolt. The way she moved and the heels on her feet were absolutely breathtaking to his eyes.

Finished with the items, Henry walked the path toward the woman as she stood at the cash register, prepared to take any customers intent on checking out.

As he walked, his eyes scanned everything about her. She had a wedding ring on her left ring finger, a pair of hoop earrings in her ears, her skin was pale white, she had blue eyes, and her smile was spectacular.

He looked down as he moved closer. Her ankles were thin, and her shoes looked new. She was the perfect target for him.

Getting up to the checkout, he began to put the items on the black rubber belt that would move them to her to scan and bag, while he continued to stare at her. She looked up to see him and smiled, "Having a good day?"

"Excellent."

"Glad to hear it," she replied, scanning the foods and bagging them up before turning to calculate the cost. She turned and told him the price, watching as he flicked a hundred-dollar bill to her. She smiled her rosy way and entered the money into the system, opening the drawer to give him his change, and handing it to him.

Henry smiled and took it, caressing her skin as he did.

Oh yeah, she was perfect. She was the kind of woman who could provide a challenge for his hunt. He was going to have a field day when he found the time to add her to his list. The idea crossed his mind repeatedly as he looked over her face while she smiled at him. He rarely found himself toying with the idea of hunting and acquiring a new addition during a random visit to the store. Most of the women that he saw or interacted with seemed like regular people, but there was something about this woman that just made him excited.

Henry smiled. "Have a good day."

"You too, sir." She nodded, watching as he left. He was a nice guy. He seemed to be one of the nicer people that she had encountered that day. Plus, she couldn't help but feel he was checking her out. Not bad, she was still surprised that she managed to catch eyes even after marrying her longtime boyfriend.

She knew the foundation would work. The two of them had been together for a while and after he'd kicked the meth habit, she knew that the pair of them would make a future together that nobody could break. It was what dreams were built on—strong beginnings.

Outside of the store, Henry placed the groceries in the backseat and got in the car before he started for home. He would be coming back soon enough. He just had to find a night when he could go on his hunt and take a detour from the red light district. He never usually hunted from the community, but rather the outskirts and fringes of the city itself. He liked it. It made him feel like he was going out of his comfort zone.

Sally would be happy that he'd actually bought everything that she'd asked him to grab, especially since he had a habit of forgetting things. She was way too sweet on him to ever truly be mad.

Oh, if only she'd treat him like trash, it might keep him from having to fantasize about other women. Especially if she wore the purple pumps while doing it.

Some things were just dreams, and life went on, at least for some. He had tried in the past to get Sally to talk down and be cruel to him, but to no avail. Even during sex, he had suggested that she take a dominant role in a few of their encounters, but it was just no use. Sally was too much of a submissive when it came to any form of D/S roleplay.

Reaching into his pocket, Henry pulled out a cigarette from the container and lit up, quickly rolling down the window in an attempt to lessen the amount of smoke in the car. He knew that Sally did not like the smell of smoke in the car, nor did she approve of him smoking, especially since she was a bit of a health nut.

Fuck that shit.

As he smoked the cig and drove the car toward his neighborhood, Henry couldn't help but picture Emily from the store: the way she looked, the way her feet looked in the heels, the way everything about her seemed to be attractive in a way that very few women ever were.

Even Sally.

She would make for an excellent Trophy, and her shoes would be perfect additions to his collection, especially if he got the chance to picture her feet modeling the shoes while he touched himself. He fumbled with the cigarette butt between his fingers as he considered the way he would stalk, hunt, take and earn what he wanted from her.

Soon, he thought to himself, soon.

CHAPTER TEN

Lifting the third slice of pizza from the box, Dr. Black took a bite and enjoyed the cheesy goodness that seemed to overwhelm his taste buds. He'd already consumed two slices without thinking; however, this time he wanted to enjoy every bite of the one he had.

The deliveryman had actually brought the pizza in record time. It was nothing short of a miracle, especially since the roads were usually packed at this hour and everyone seemed to be on the go.

At least, he hoped that was what was keeping his helpers from showing up in the allotted hour or so that he had been expecting them. After this was said and done, he'd probably have to dispose of them like he did the driver who collected the aborted fetus corpses.

He didn't like having to kill the help, but as he had said before, sacrifices had to be made for the greater good. At least that was the excuse he was giving himself. *People.*

He shook his head. *People were just so unreliable when you needed them the most.*

As he went to take another bite of the slice of pizza, he heard the sound of knuckles rapping on the warehouse door. He groaned and set the slice back in the box, wiping his mouth on his sleeve before heading toward the door. Gripping the handle before twisting and pulling the door open slightly, Black peered through the crack to see Rory and his brother, Malcolm, standing at the entrance.

"It's about time," Black said before pulling the door open and allowing the two to enter the warehouse. Rory, the larger of the pair, nodded. "Sorry about the delay. We had to deal with some shit and–"

"I don't care about excuses," Black hissed while slamming the door shut and turning to the pair. "The sun is setting soon, and I need the two of you to carry out an assignment for me."

The loud slam of the door being shut forced the brothers to jump slightly. They watched as the doctor walked past them towards the table of beakers before turning to face them. He placed his hands together and smiled slyly, "I'll pay you both three hundred for the job."

"Three hundred?" Malcolm's eyes lit up. "What do we gotta do? Another mail-order pickup?"

"Not this time." Black chuckled. "I need you to go on a search-and-take mission."

The brothers looked at each other and then back at the scientist before Rory tilted his head, "Huh?"

Black nodded as he chose his words carefully. "I need you guys to procure test subjects for my experimental formula. The test subjects must be alive and have no physical defects; I want them to be in as good a shape as you can find. I want at least twenty of them."

"Test subjects? Like puppies or rabbits?"

"No." Black laughed at the suggestion. The fools had previously thought he was creating a new lip balm, and animal testing was all the rage for beauty products, but he thought he'd made it clear that he wasn't doing that. Shaking his head, he straightened up and said, "No, I need babies."

The two brothers immediately dropped their jaws in both horror and shock. They'd had a feeling that the doctor was not in the right state of mind, especially since he seemed to be doing all of his work outside the normal parameters of what they imagined a testing facility would look like, but this was something else entirely. Malcolm closed his mouth and swallowed. "Like human babies?"

"Precisely."

"And where exactly are we supposed to find babies for you to use as test subjects?"

"You don't watch the news very much, do you? This city is full of babies that have been cast out, tossed in the trash cans by unfit parents or single people who thought that their spouse would stick around if they had a child. It's a fucking tragedy, really, but in this case I'm thankful for it."

"Holy fuck." Rory shuddered at the thought of a baby being abandoned in a trash can. People were so fucking terrible to do such a thing. It was inhuman. He looked at the doctor as he spoke, bottom lip trembling, "May I ask what exactly you plan to do with the babies?"

"Hmm..." Black rubbed his chin as he pondered the question. The two of them had been very helpful thus far, plus he knew they might need a little more push to get the job done, and he wasn't the best at lying. He shrugged, "My experiment is a formula that will improve the brains of infants. It will increase their ability to think and talk; they'll be able to communicate their needs with their parents, caregivers, etcetera. I want to feed my formula to the test subjects that you two will procure and see if I need to add or subtract any ingredients from the concoction. The babies will be taken care of and they'll even gain intelligence far beyond that of any other infant; it's all part of the plan."

"A drug to increase a baby's smarts? Say..." Malcolm nodded in approval. "I like the sound of that."

"It's a brilliant idea, right?"

"Sure is." Malcolm nodded while turning to an unsure Rory and then back to the doctor. "Okay, Doc, I think we can fill your request."

"Huh?" Rory looked at his brother with wide eyes. Rory couldn't help but wonder what would happen if the serum didn't work or caused the test subjects to be overwhelmed by side effects; however, he could tell that Malcolm would not hear any of it. Malcolm nodded at him. "This sounds like a hell of an idea. Remember how I'm always saying I won't have kids cuz all they do is whine? Well, if this shit works, I might be able to stomach having some brats."

Before Rory could respond, Black looked up from rubbing his eyes in annoyance and asked, "So, do you think you guys can get this job done before midnight?"

"Not a problem, boss." Malcolm nodded. "Just one thing. Do you know where to look for the subjects?"

Black shrugged. "Anywhere. Look in the trash cans near hospitals, fire departments, police stations, hell, look in the city park. You should be able to fill the quota in no time."

"Do you want us to grab anything else? Milk or baby food or something?"

"Sure." Black dug a hundred-dollar bill from his coat pocket and handed it to the brothers. "Get all that shit. We want to ensure our test subjects are provided for, after all."

"True story." Malcolm nodded before taking the wrinkly bill from the scientist and turned to his brother, "You ready to go?"

"I'm still not sure about this," Rory replied, "What if the experiments don't work?"

Black raised his hand to silence him. "Now, now; we don't need that kind of negativity. I've taken care of every step and precaution. The formula will work wonders. I'll show you once you get me what I need. Now, go and make sure you follow my order to the detail. I need living and perfect specimens, no defects or flaws that will impede the formula."

"Say no more, we're on our way," Malcolm replied before grabbing his brother's shirt and pulling the big guy out of the building, closing the door behind them. Black couldn't help but burst out laughing once the pair had exited. *Stupid people.*

He shook his head and turned back to the table, looking down at the completed formula. Those ingrates would complete his step, and then, he'd probably send them on a mission to retrieve drugs before he called the cops in advance. They'd get prison and be out of his hair, everything wrapped up in a neat little package.

Reaching over to retrieve the slice of pizza he'd been savoring, Black took another bite and smiled as he let it satiate his taste buds. It was almost as delicious as the idea of victory.

Victory never tasted so sweet.

Chapter Eleven

Stephanie looked through the piles of folders that she had pulled from the filing office and sat at the table. She had spent the entire day searching through every known case tied to the Foot Carver.

It was no small feat.

The files had been organized—thank God for that—except everything seemed to be disjointed when it came to establishing a pattern for the killer. Sipping her twelfth or thirteenth cup of coffee for the day, Stephanie took another deep dive into a case file that was splayed out before her on the table. She swiftly studied every line, every bit of text, and every element of the crime scene as it had been recorded by the detective who handled it.

The said detective was no longer on the force, effectively rendering this particular case cold.

Stephanie jotted down notes that she recorded in her mind for good measure, ensuring that everything would be touched on and nothing would be missed when she decided to finally assess the entire situation. However, this particular case ended after the crime scene was cleared and no further investigation was concluded—no doubt because of other "pressing" matters for the detective who was handling it.

He had been connected to one of the local syndicates, Triads, maybe. She couldn't recall at this particular juncture, but all she knew was that he'd been kicked off the force for murdering a potential witness to an upcoming trial and not one fuck had been given. He was probably rotting in a jail cell or living it up on an island somewhere.

Justice rarely got served in the city.

It made everything seem a bit futile in the mechanics of police work, but that was just how the powers that be saw fit for it to go down. She couldn't think about that now and grabbed another folder to open, immediately facing down the image of a woman missing her head and feet. The head had been located a block from the crime scene. Semen found on the tongue was a foul fact that revealed why he'd taken the decapitated head with him.

However, the semen sample had been lost or misplaced, tax money hard at work.

Sitting back and sighing, Stephanie couldn't help but realize that the mishandling of everything seemed to ensure that the Killer always got away with the crime. Hell, at this point, it was a surprise that more people weren't out hacking and slashing people to death, especially since the cops were utterly incompetent when it came to actually doing their job.

Rubbing the brow of her forehead, Stephanie finished her coffee, and that's when she realized she hadn't looked at her watch the entire day. Looking down, she was a bit surprised to learn that it was already eight in the evening and she'd been perusing file after file for her entire workday.

Turning to see the mountain of files still waiting to be cracked, she knew there was no chance she could get through them on overtime, especially since the chief was getting antsy about officers overusing and abusing the shifts. The files would still be there in the morning, and she would have a clear head to further discover the stupidity of her fellow officers.

Closing the file she had opened and setting it aside, Stephanie stood from the desk before heading out of the filing office. Heading back to her own office, she passed uniformed officers in the hall and caught sight of a few petty hoods being hauled in for questioning for some obscure crime.

This was the way that the daily toil of police work went in the city. Half the time, criminals went in and came right back out as though a revolving door had been installed in the front of the department building. There was always something going on in the city: there were gangs, syndicates, organized dealers, and always a rash of carjackings that never ended.

Money was the only thing that mattered at the end of the day, and people were willing to do anything to acquire it.

Stephanie finally reached her office and proceeded to grab her bag, realizing she'd completely missed lunch when she took note of the small lunch box resting within. Damn, she hadn't been that deeply engrossed in something since long before the Henderson case. The Foot Carver had her brain pumping more than ever before, and she loved every minute of it.

Turning off the light in her office, Stephanie closed the door and started walking toward the entrance of the department building. Moving quickly past everyone else, she briefly heard Collins' smug voice wishing her a goodnight and made it out of the building, taking a breath of the city's thick air. The street was packed with cars moving back and forth, occasionally trying to cut each other off as the overcast weather started drizzling rain from the heavens above.

Stephanie quickly turned and moved toward her car, fishing her keys out of her jacket before unlocking the vehicle. Opening the door, she placed the bag in the passenger seat and got in, closing the door to beat the heavy rain from pelting her. She gripped the steering wheel as she watched the rain pouring onto the windshield and closed her eyes, her mind still in deep focus over everything she had read during the shift.

Every case file, every report, and every crime scene photo was swimming around in her head like a horror collage. The details of the bodies being mutilated, their feet being hacked off along with the occasional hand, head, or breast, it was all fascinating to her. She had only read about that kind of stuff in books and seen it in films, but she was living in a city where a person was proactively performing such sadistic activities on anyone and everyone.

It was bizarre and yet, seemingly surreal for her. Stephanie knew crime was a never-ending nightmare for the city, but the thought that a wildly active serial killer was prowling the streets at night, hunting and hacking up his prey like a true-to-life monster, was just overwhelming. She felt her heart racing at the idea.

Opening her eyes, she took a deep breath and stuck the key in the ignition, turning over the engine before pulling on her seatbelt. Looking behind her despite the rearview mirror being in perfect condition, she backed up the car from its parking space and kicked it into drive, exiting the parking lot for the open road back to her apartment.

Looking out the window as she drove through the street, she saw the buildings that were half-lit and half-dark, her mind wondering if he was in one of them. If not him, what other serial killer or freak of nature was nesting in the drab apartments and slums of the city?

And how long would it be before they struck?

Stopping at a red light before her turnoff, Stephanie saw a large delivery truck pulling up to the curb and parking before another man got out to open the lids of the trash cans. She watched them with a cocked eyebrow. They weren't trash collectors, and the street light revealed the logo on the side of the delivery truck.

Suggs Bros. Imports

She watched with slight intensity as the smaller guy continued to search through the silver trash cans, pulling out various items before he paused. He raised his head to look around slightly before reaching down to grasp something from within. However, the darkness of the night evaded her ability to see what he was carrying before he got back into the cab of the truck.

By this point, a loud horn filled the air as Stephanie realized the light had turned green and she was holding up traffic. Slowly, she pressed on the gas pedal and advanced down the road, doing her best to get a look at the two in the delivery truck's cab before driving past them. She hadn't heard of that company before, and while digging through the trash wasn't exactly a crime, it could have easily been a drug search.

Shaking her head, she cleared the idea from her mind. She had to focus on the Foot Carver. She couldn't let herself get carried away with penny-ante bullshit anymore. She had to put together the pattern that kept the monster going.

It was her case now, and she was going to solve it, especially since it puzzled her more than anything else.

Chapter Twelve

Rumbling along in the delivery truck, Malcolm and Rory were overwhelmed with the constant crying of infants they had managed to find in the city trash cans. Malcolm groaned, he hated the sound that children made when they were upset or hungry or whatever the fuck.

Trying to cover his ears agaiinst the constant crying, he shouted to his brother, "Goddamn, I hope the doctor gets that formula patented and mass-produced. I don't know how bitches put up with this shit nonstop!"

Rory remained silent. He was still battling the idea of finding and giving infants to the doctor for whatever scientific purposes he had in store for them. He didn't like the idea of trafficking the babies for some convoluted experiment. Malcolm screamed, "Please shut up!"

Finally, they pulled up to another curb outside of a local firehouse, and Rory parked the truck. Malcolm silently thanked whatever God there was that he didn't have to put up with the constant whining for a matter of minutes. Small miracles.

Getting out of the cab, Malcolm stepped over to the shiny silver trash can, its lid callously placed on the rim, and lifted it to view the contents. Almost immediately, he was caught off guard by two toddlers who stared back at him with wonder and curiosity. Thank God, he thought to himself, at least these two were not in a state of panic, and whatever else was bothering the others.

The two toddlers seemed almost placated by his appearance.

Inside the truck, Rory turned in his seat to look in the back and saw the various faces of the crying, abandoned infants, hungry for attention. They were covered in filth, each of them in need of some kind of nourishment, and they all seemed to be focused on getting some kind of affection.

His heart hurt as he imagined how terrifying this all must have been for them. It was so cruel that anyone could just up and abandon their newborn in a trash can to be exposed to the elements.

At least the doctor had promised that the babies would be taken care of and provided for while also being part of his experiment. Rory attempted to find some solace in that, even if he personally didn't believe that Dr. Black would follow through on his word.

The man was greedy and seemed to be out for his own success. It would be a total surprise if he followed through on his promise to the brothers.

Outside, Malcolm slowly raised both toddlers out of the trash can with his hands and held them against his chest as he ventured toward the back of the delivery truck. Raising his foot to kick the handle, he did his best to grip and lift the door enough for him to place the toddlers within. Slowly, the two little ones climbed off him and crawled into the back of the truck, despite the array of screaming and silent infants that seemed to be intent on destroying his sanity.

Doing his best not to scream at them all at the top of his lungs, Malcolm counted every one of the little bundles of joy as best he could. By some small miracle, they'd managed to find the required number, and the toddlers provided an extra two.

Maybe they could get a bonus for the pair?

Closing the lid of the trunk and turning to rest against it, Malcolm groaned in utter annoyance at the shrill whining of the "test subjects". He hated babies. They were literally the worst part of the human life cycle.

He couldn't stand old people either for much of the same reason, but at least they slept ninety percent of the time.

Walking away from the back of the truck, Malcolm headed back into the cab and rejoined his brother as the nonstop crying flooded the peaceful existence of his mind. He looked at him. "Get us the fuck back to the warehouse."

"Do we have enough?"

"More than enough." Malcolm nodded. "if I ever see another little shit again, I'll shoot myself in the ballsack."

"They're not that bad." Rory shook his head and started up the truck, turning onto the street to head for the warehouse. He didn't want to do it. He wanted to take the babies somewhere they could be taken care of. They deserved a home like everyone else. Hell, they deserved a home *more* than everyone else. They were innocent in all of this, and yet, he was driving them towards a destination he wasn't sure they would make it out of.

Looking at his brother, Rory swallowed. "So, how many did we find?"

"Like twenty-two."

"Wow," Rory feigned surprise as he drove along, listening to the screeches and cries from the babies in the back. "So we don't technically need to give him two of them."

"What?" Malcolm looked at his brother with a look of both shock and disgust. "What are you—no—Ror, we're not keeping any of them."

Rory sighed, "I'm just saying these kids need someone to take care of them, and they don't have anyone in their lives."

"Yes, they do," Malcolm countered. "They have a scientist who's going to make them smart and give them a better chance at life. We're a pair of idiots who couldn't even manage the company our parents left us, you really think we can take care of a fucking infant?"

"I'm willing to try if you are."

"I'm not, and neither are you," Malcolm replied. "Now, shut the fuck up and drive the truck. I hear one more word about keeping one of these little fucks and I'm gonna sell you to the scientist for some brains."

Dejected, Rory simply continued with the drive and listened to the pained cries of the infants in the back of the truck. He wanted to knock Malcolm out, take the kids back to their family home, and forget the whole job. He wanted to give each of them a chance they wouldn't get otherwise.

He never knew the city was full of abandoned and discarded children. He'd seen street urchins running here and there during the delivery days, but he never imagined that there were that many infants disposed of and left to the elements of the city and its unhinged inhabitants. The whole realization put a knot in his stomach as he contemplated helping more in the future.

He wanted to help the ones currently in his charge.

Alas, all he had to go on was Dr. Black's word, and as much as he didn't want to, he had to trust the man. There wasn't anything else he could do about the situation at hand.

Pulling off the main street, he continued onward until they entered a slum district on the way toward the warehouse. Looking out the windows, Rory saw the massive amounts of silver trash cans and bins that lined the streets.

All he could think of was how many of them had babies casually dumped within, fighting for their lives, wondering what happened to their mother's loving embrace.

Chapter Thirteen

Henry cruised the dark streets in the car, watching the road light in uneven spaces between each streetlight.

The air was cold, and the sky was jet black, covered by clouds of looming fright. No moon or stars would shine on this night. It was the perfect night for him to take care of the needs that had been burning in his mind all day. He hadn't planned on going hunting again this early, but he couldn't get the fantasy of Emily out of his mind, and he didn't want to lose the urge.

He had to get his woman. He had to find and conquer his prey. It was forcing him to take the matter to heart, and when that happened, there was no stopping him from following through with it.

Henry couldn't help but feel a slight burn of excitement in his groin. The idea of taking down Emily, the cashier, was going to be a turn-on. She had beautiful feet and an excellent pair of tits, definitely something to drool over, much like the women he fantasized about in his youth.

Plus, she had the shoes to boot.

Pulling up in the empty lot outside of the store, Henry sat with the engine off and his eyes focused on the electric double doors, eager for the employees to start heading home.

Taking the blade from his coat pocket, he raised it to catch the light glaring from the parking lot lights, burning or flashing as their bulbs sought the last bit of energy to illuminate the area. This part of town was drastically in need of assistance.

The whole city was in desperate need of assistance. It could probably do with a nuclear bomb and cleanup. Then, there would be less crime and more progress made for the benefit of society.

The lights within the store dimmed, and the employees began to exit, some going to their cars while others opted for a walk to their homes a short distance away. It just so happened that Emily, the round-faced babe with the big titties and pretty feet, was walking to her apartment complex around the corner of the block next to the store. It made for a short distance and saved on the luxury of gas, plus the air was usually pretty still for her to be out in.

Tonight it was cold and rainy. The city tended to always be overcast with rain, fog, or something to make life just that much more difficult. Smart people would move on with their lives and find a new place to live, but no, people from the city knew it was the best place to be. It was an asylum for people like him.

Maybe you really had to be crazy to live in such a horrible place.

Henry got out of the car, crouching to watch as she walked away from her coworkers and headed for her trail. His breathing provided a bit of visible fog to roll from his lips. He was horny. He could feel himself harden as he watched her saunter away.

She was better than the hookers and the college girls. She was fresh and looked like a piece of fresh meat, teasing him for what he needed from her.

Getting up and walking out of the illuminating glow of street lights, Henry walked a few yards from her, preparing himself for the inevitable chase. She wouldn't run far or fast, but she would definitely give him a run for the catch—a challenge of sport.

He liked it.

He desired it.

She was a piece of meat, and he was a lion, prepared to claim his prize by taking her out in the darkness. He trailed after her as she crossed the desolate street and continued on the sidewalk, her hands in her denim jacket that had been placed over her shoulders.

Taking out the knife, he immediately started jogging toward her, moving on his toes to reduce the amount of sound that he would make in his movements. She paused to turn around and screamed upon seeing his dark figure zooming towards her; however, Emily was not one to be made a victim. Swinging her purse, she struck Henry in the face, knocking him to the cold pavement as she turned to send the toe of her pump into his ribs.

Henry cried out, getting stomped and kicked by the woman, her feet moving quicker than he could imagine.

The heel of her pump caught into the side of his face, tearing his cheek open and forcing blood to flow from it with every beat of his heart. He loved it. He couldn't help but release a cringing laugh that cackled through the air. He felt ready to burst in his pants as the realization of a woman beating him with her shoes was enough to make his dreams a reality.

This was what he wanted for so long.

She screamed, "I'll call the police! I'll call for help! Don't fuck with me!"

His mind coming back to the clarity of the moment, Henry quickly grabbed the handle of the knife and swung upward, cleaving a gash moving up her thigh. She screamed out in pain, blood pulsing from the open wound as she attempted to move back from him, reaching down to feel how bad the damage was.

This was it. He wouldn't get another shot.

Henry rose to his feet, swinging the blade and slashing across her gut as she dropped her purse, she screamed out in abject terror. Immediately, she turned to run, only for him to grab the back of her jacket whilst yanking her into the alley between the apartment complex and a small shop.

Forcing her way out of the jacket, Emily attempted to make a break for it, only for Henry to throw himself towards her and swipe the blade into her heel. The physical attempt to stand upon the slashed tendon forced her body to shift weight, and with a sickening screech, she fell to the ground on her side. Emily attempted to drag herself to the sidewalk, her once-manicured nails now tearing and breaking while she pulled herself along, the ground covered in trash, rat shit and dirty needles.

Henry was on top of her in an instant, the woman attempting to punch and swing her hands at him. Her attempts to get him away were sadly futile as he used his grip to tear her floral dress open down the middle.

Instantly, her pale skin was revealed in the dim light of the street lamps across from them.

Shock had encapsulated her body, and she was no longer fighting him, her body being violated enough to break her survival skills.

Henry didn't care. She had fulfilled his fantasy, and now, he needed to fulfill the contract. Taking the blade, he looked down at her face as she stared at him with the deepest hatred he had ever seen in anyone's eyes. He swung the cold steel in the dim light of the street lamps and opened her throat wide for her crimson to burst forth all around her. The dark blood pooled around her body as the life-force escaped her physical form and left behind only her corpse to stare at him, no life behind the eyes anymore.

Reaching into his pocket, Henry pulled out his trusted trash bag and unfurled it, preparing to get to work on his needed obligations.

Slowly, he cleaved the blade at the base of her left breast and carved through the muscle and viscera, leaving a large empty chunk of visible wet muscle from beneath. Acting fast, he removed the other as well.. She had beautiful tits.

Moving from her mutilated torso, Henry planted his lips down her legs, biting her thighs and licking around her kneecaps until he reached her feet.

Thankfully, one was already practically removed thanks to the lucky slash of the Achilles tendon. He only had to swing a few times and finish the job, jaggedly hacking her foot from her leg. The blood poured rapidly from the wound and coated the hard ground in warm, wet, copper fluid.

Henry smiled and licked his lips as he hacked repeatedly through the limb. Twisting the bone with a sickening crunch, the serial killer ripped his trophy from the rest of the leg.

Beautiful.

Placing the detached foot in the bag with the set of breasts, Henry worked on doing the same to the other foot, removing it in gloriously bloody form and twisting it off, breaking the bone into pieces in the process.

Filling his bag, he next picked up her pumps and held them in the light provided by the street lamps, looking them over. His eyes danced around their make and setup, and the way they seemed to glow in front of his pupils.

Setting the blade in his pocket and moving the bag to the side, Henry rose to his feet whilst holding the shoes beneath his cock. It was limp, yet he knew it would be hard soon, and he set to work, stroking himself while looking down at the shoes. They were so beautiful, so glorious, so utterly remarkable.

His balls tightened as he jerked harder and quicker, eager to reach his climax to splash all over the pumps.

He growled, angrily moaning while looking down at the make of the pump, the figure of them being something he had seen a thousand times, and yet, it was like the first time he had ever seen them at all. He raised them to his nose and inhaled, the smell of her skin lotion mixed with the sweat of all-day working was enough to get him to reach his peak.

Quickly, he moved them under his tool and dropped his release upon the sleek interior of the lady's shoes. Taking a heavy sigh, he placed them in the bag and tied it off, making sure to zip up his cock. It was still dripping, but he didn't mind it; at least it wasn't acid or something.

Looking down at Emily's butchered state, he couldn't help but smile. She had been such a giggly woman. She was a good fuck and a great dominatrix, even if she hadn't wanted to be either; she was exactly what he wanted.

Hopefully, her man, if she had one, could find another woman who was as much of a freak as she was.

Henry carried his trophies back down the sidewalk as he walked back to his car. He'd be up all night in his man-cave, fixing up resin molds of the feet and tits. He breathed in the cold air and released it as visible air from his mouth. This was the kind of night he lived for.

CHAPTER FOURTEEN

The blender ran quickly, reducing the contents within the heavy glass pitcher to little more than a pureed watery mixture, the color of which was a light brown. Dr. Black removed the lid and poured the thick mix into a small bowl that he placed next to the beaker of his formula.

It was nearing midnight, and the Suggs brothers were still out retrieving his specimens, much to his growing annoyance. He couldn't help but tap his fingers impatiently on the table as he waited for them to return.

The weight had been almost impossible to sit through. After all, the news made it sound like there was a baby in every trash can in the city. Maybe it wasn't nearly as widespread as he'd been led to believe?

Rolling his eyes, he turned to look at the bloody blender and chuckled. The driver's body had proved to be an excellent source of delivery. The formula would have to be delivered into the mix, and since there was a shortage of applicable baby food in the warehouse, the doctor figured that composting the corpse of his former Pickup Man would be a wise decision. So far, he'd been proven right about everything else.

After all, the specimens would be starving and liable to consume anything with questionable nutritional value attached.

Suddenly, the sound of a truck pulling up outside the warehouse caught his attention, and Black turned quickly with a smile pulling on his lips. The fuckers were finally back with his test subjects!

Moving toward the door, the scientist buttoned up his dirty lab coat and pressed the button on the remote to raise the heavy metal door for truck deliveries. The rattling of the door filled the building as it slowly creaked and shuddered until it was open enough to allow the subjects to be brought in. Black watched with slight impatience as the delivery truck backed up to the landing and parked before the brothers exited the cab, both looking like they had been through a warzone.

"Did you find what I asked?" Black hissed.

Malcolm put his hands on his hips and nodded. "You best believe it! We found twenty-two little patients, and trust me, they are in serious need of a brain adjustment!"

Black rubbed his hands together and nodded with a hint of malice on his face. "Perfect, now bring them in and I'll get your fees."

"No problem," Malcolm replied before gesturing to his brother and watching as the larger Rory opened the back of the truck. The non-stop whining and crying had died down to a dull whimper by that point. Most of the babies had fallen asleep thanks to the peaceful ride in the back of the moving vehicle.

It was weird how that worked, but Malcolm was not one to question a good thing.

Slowly, the two brothers removed each child from within the back of the truck and placed them on the dirty blanket that Dr. Black had laid out on the floor beside the workplace he'd set up for the experiment. It wasn't much, but it was comfortable enough for the babies to remain in their hardened slumber.

Rory placed the babies in rows of four while ensuring not to jostle them awake. His heart continued to hurt as he fought internally with placing them in the care of the mad doctor they were assisting. He couldn't help but fight the urge to take them back home and give them a life they deserved, even if he knew he'd never be able to afford every need they desired.

Malcolm, on the other hand, sat the babies down on the blanket in no specific order and thanked his lucky stars that he wouldn't have to be around any of them ever again. This particular job had been grating on his nerves, and he was out of patience for them, the doctor and his brother's bleeding heart. All he wanted at this point was to get the fuck back home and go to bed, especially since he knew the back of the delivery truck would have to be cleaned from all the baby shit that was no doubt caked on the floor.

Dr. Black watched the brothers deliver the babies on the blanket he'd laid on the floor and chuckled; they were almost competent enough to receive a bonus for everything they'd done. Almost.

Looking down at the faces of the infants on the floor, he couldn't help but wonder just how incredible they would be after the experiment worked its magic. They would be able to speak and relay their needs in applicable words; it would be absolutely incredible to see. The infants were largely covered in old newspapers or tattered onesies that had been ruined by the elements. All of them were filthy, and the majority of them were thin and gangly.

It really must have been hell being thrown into a trash can and forced to fend for themselves, especially in a city where people didn't bother to take care of themselves, much less each other. Indeed, such a tragedy.

It was then that Black saw Rory bringing in two toddlers in his arms, both of them had light brown hair and beady black eyes. He growled, "I told you idiots to bring me infants, not toddlers!"

"Huh?" Malcolm looked at the scientist. "Same thing, ain't they?"

"No!" Black screamed, the raised voice forcing some of the infants to startle awake and begin crying aloud as their needs were made known within themselves. Stomping toward the Suggs brothers, Black raised his finger at them and then at the toddlers who stared at him. "Toddler brains are already on the way toward development. Infant brains are piles of mush. I can't get an accurate reading if I give the serum to the toddlers. I don't want them!"

"Doc, I'm sorry," Malcolm apologized while raising his hands. "What do you want us to do with them?"

"I don't care, dispose of them." Black threw his hands in the air as he turned toward the experiment workspace, "Throw them back in the trash where you found them."

"NO!" Rory screamed loud enough to force all of the infants and toddlers to cry out in fear.

Black turned around to face the man. "No?"

"You can't send them back! You promised you'd take care of them, so do it!"

Black tilted his head at the large man. He knew the big lug was soft at heart. It was made perfectly clear by that point. His look of disgust twisted into a look of feigned care before he nodded swiftly, "Very well, Mr. Suggs, maybe I can find some use for them in the experiment's proceedings. Will that make you happy?"

"It will," Rory replied. "But I better not find them on the street or else."

"Or else what?" Black asked while cocking his right eyebrow. Rory started toward the man, but was quickly pulled back by his brother, who shook his head. "Now, now, let's not get carried away. We did our part, and I think it's best if we let the doctor get on with his experiment."

"Good idea," Black replied before stretching out his hand with an envelope for the pair. Malcolm took the fat envelope and smiled. "Pleasure doing business with you, doc, let us know how the experiment goes. Let's go, Rory."

Rory continued to stare daggers at the scientist as his brother attempted to pull him out of the warehouse toward the truck. He felt a burning urge to tear the man's head clear off his shoulders and save the children from whatever hell was waiting for them in the man's care. However, he finally turned around and headed out the door with his brother pulling him along to avoid any further conflict that might unravel.

Black watched the pair leave and silently gnashed his teeth, the pistol in the pocket of his lab coat only inches from his hand. He could have very easily pulled it out and ended the big bastard with little effort. It wouldn't have been a problem for him. After all, there was no place in this business for wimps and bleeding hearts.

Once the pair got in the truck and exited the premises, Black hurriedly pressed the button on the remote to bring the door down until it sealed shut. The warehouse was secure, the night was late, and the babies were screaming aloud. It was absolutely riveting for him. The scientist could feel his heart ready to burst with excitement as he turned and looked down at each of the little test subjects.

"Now–" He smiled slyly. "It's feeding time."

Chapter Fifteen

The night continued as Dr. Black quickly cleared the first table of everything that could cause a hindrance to the procedure, his mind swimming with the ideas that continued to pour in from his brain. He was so close to seeing the experiment come to fruition.

He had the setup, the hypothesis in motion, the activity prepped for actual action, and now, he had more than enough specimens for testing. This was the kind of thing that he fucking lived for.

Finally, all that was left on the table was the bowl of pureed flesh and a syringe filled with a few cubic centimeters of the formula he'd spent so long creating. Turning to the *work* table, he looked over everything before selecting a spoon to feed the mix and brought it to the *operating* table. He couldn't help but chuckle at the thought of giving his tables little designations.

Had to have fun with it, he chuckled to himself.

Immediately, he turned and scanned over the subjects with his eyes on the floor as he considered which one would be the prime example to start with. He had twenty-two to choose from, and the first one could always prove to be fatal, so it would be ideal to start with one of the subjects he wouldn't mind losing.

The toddlers were the obvious choice.

Getting down on one knee, he eyed the two toddlers and clapped his hands. "Hey."

The toddlers looked over at him with one of them giggling at the sound of the clapping and the other simply staring. He chuckled. "Mr. Giggles."

Yes, he would be the first pick.

Bingo.

Reaching out, he lifted the giggling toddler in his hands and turned toward the operating table before placing the little guy on the surface. Black took the syringe from beside the bowl and proceeded to slowly press the plunger as he held the needle over the thick mix of flesh and water. The serum dripped out of the needle into the mix before the scientist ceased his action and placed the syringe back down, pulling out his notepad to scribble down the activity.

Taking the spoon in hand, he slowly mixed the contents of the bowl and watched as the makeshift food turned into a porous paste that stuck to the spoon as he stirred it. It didn't look appetizing to him, but to a starving child, it probably looked like a dream come true.

Taking a bit of the paste on the spoon, he raised it towards the toddler, who was busy looking around the room and rubbing his head. Black smiled. "Now, open the airplane."

The toddler's small mouth opened as Black pushed the spoon slowly into the little one's mouth and watched as he consumed it, taking no time at all to clean the spoon from sheer hunger. Mr. Giggles, to Black's surprise, was hardly fazed by the taste of the paste and giggled again. Smiling widely, the scientist took another small bit of the paste on the spoon and proceeded to feed it to the child.

It was almost like a bonding moment, and Black couldn't help but feel proud of his ability to properly feed a child. The screaming and crying of the others on the floor was drowned out by the look on Mr. Giggles's face as his eyes lit up from being fed for the first time in a while. It was heartwarming. The whole situation, Black thought, was difficult to explain in words, but he'd do his best when writing the speech for his Nobel Prize.

After a few more spoonfuls of the paste, Black noticed that Mr. Giggles looked at him in a way that seemed to be almost confused. Setting the spoon into the bowl, he looked at the boy and said, "What?"

The toddler's eyes stared at the man as though studying him. Something seemed off. Taking the notepad in hand, Black scribbled the change in behavior on the paper and cleared his throat before speaking slowly. "Are you okay?"

Mr. Giggles' confused face quickly changed to a smile, and a giggling fit overtook the little creation. Breathing a sigh of annoyance, Black groaned. He'd hoped for something a little more intelligent than simply a game of childish humor. Shaking his head, Black threw the notepad on the table and turned away from the child to look down at the rest of the screaming infants on the floor.

Their noisy little mouths were open constantly, whining and whimpering and begging for nourishment. He couldn't help but feel that twenty charges might have been too big an order, especially since he didn't have nearly enough blankets or comforts for them. He'd hoped the formula would take an instant effect, and he'd at least be able to get them to speak, but the first subject had proved to be a failure.

He looked at the bowl of paste and growled. It must have been the food. Perhaps, he needed a more direct approach to delivering the serum.

Grasping the syringe from the table, he quickly bent over the toddler and hoisted the needle over the back of Mr. Giggles' neck. Looking over the space, he eyed the place where the spine connected to the brain stem and, with a soft push, inserted the needle into the skin.

Almost immediately, Mr. Giggles began to scream and cry from the shock of being stuck with a needle. Black growled, "Keep quiet, it'll be over soon enough."

Pressing on the plunger, he watched as the liquid pressed through the needle directly into the child's brain stem. The anger beaming off of him was more than enough to drown out the cries of the toddler in his grip. Once he'd injected enough, he pulled the needle out and released Mr. Giggles, watching as the toddler fell back flat on the table before him.

Setting the syringe on the table, Black breathed hard as he watched the toddler's body lie still and lifeless. He swallowed and shook his head, his slicked back hair managed to hang over his forehead before he pushed it back with annoyance. Sniffing, he whispered, "Mr. Giggles?"

The toddler's lifeless body remained still on the table. Black sighed, "Shit, Mr. Giggles, can you hear me?"

Silence emanated from the little one's body as Black ran his hands through his hair. He should have had patience.

He should have waited. The results could have taken place over time. He didn't need to do what he'd done. He'd just killed the toddler, and it seemed like the only one in the bunch that had any personality to it. *Fuck,* he thought. *This was all a mistake.*

He knew he'd make a few here and there, but he rarely lost his temper to the point of doing something extreme. He shook his head. "Come on, I'm sorry, just please don't go out on me. Not now!"

Suddenly, Mr. Giggles' eyes shot open as the toddler's body raised to sit back up and stared at Black. The man felt a sense of relief rush over his body as he stepped back slightly, doing his best to avoid stepping on any of the infants. He looked at the toddler. "Mr. Giggles, are you okay?"

The toddler looked around the warehouse with his beady eyes, his jaw moving up and down as he studied the room and then back to the scientist. The air was surprisingly quiet and still; even the infants had lowered their cries as though time had stopped dead in its tracks. Black swallowed and watched the toddler stare at him with an intent that he couldn't quite put a finger on.

Mr. Giggles' lips slowly pulled into a soft smile before opening. "Mr. Giggles is okay."

Chapter Sixteen

After arriving at the department the next day, Stephanie made a beeline straight for the files and picked up where she left off. All night, she'd been trying to piece together some kind of factor that led the Foot Carver to continue on his spree.

Unfortunately, more factors made more sense.

Such as the fact that the police were incompetent in trying to hunt him. Plus, most of the women he chose were women who worked the red light districts that covered the city like pockmarks on an acne-ridden teen. The problem with getting any kind of help from the red light workers was all part of the street code of silence.

The city's underbelly was famous for that kind of problem.

They didn't talk to cops. It was the number one rule that seemed to be cemented into everyone's mind—no cooperation for the boys in blue. Usually, that would resort to mob justice and lynchings, but even then, the vigilantism would go unnoticed by the department.

It really made the lives of honest cops harder to handle.

Sipping her third cup of coffee, Stephanie pulled another file and opened it, noting that the date was almost four years earlier. It was one of the monster's first ten kills. She sniffed before reading over the details of the crime scene, the injuries sustained by the victim, and the overall lack of depth that the detective on the case had put into any actual work.

The time passed by slowly for her as she surveyed every case, using a notebook to jot down every little detail while simultaneously recording it in her mind for future consideration. The points of interest stemmed from the focus that the Carver put into each victim's death.

They were usually placed in a certain way, their bodies left to rot in the spot they fell without any care being given beyond the removal of feet and other extremities that the killer felt were needed. A sense of wonder fell over her mind as she contemplated the use of the limbs as trophies. It wasn't uncommon for serial killers to take trophies, usually jewelry, articles of clothing, or minor parts of the victim.

However, the situation with the Foot Carver seemed to go deeper than a simple trophy hunt. It was all some form of game for him. The way he treated the bodies of the victims after killing them. They were left without any kind of interest or care; they were simply dropped and discarded.

It was like some kind of a meager disposal.

They were nothing more than streetwalkers and good-time gals; street trash in his mind. Obviously, the Foot Carver had a sense of superiority over them. They were just animals for him to hunt as one would hunt a rat or a wild pig. Once the hunt was complete, the trophy would be taken and the carcass left to rot in the wild where it belonged.

The city was one giant wildlife preserve for the Foot Carver, and he wasn't going to stop until someone stopped him, no matter how much he wanted to—*if* he even wanted to.

Stephanie sat back and considered an idea that crossed her mind. The compulsion game was real. Once someone got into a habit and couldn't get the fire out of their gut, the compulsive need to continue was overwhelming. The Foot Carver had gotten away with it for so long because of one thing or another—it was a compulsive need to be fulfilled. The trophies and shoes were part of it.

She wrote down the notes as she worked them out. Something had occurred in the Foot Carver's past that led him to hunt feet and shoes; yet there was some other interest he had in the targets—something she couldn't put her finger on. It was another factor in his compulsion that fed into his ego and forced him to go after women in general.

Perhaps he'd had a strained relationship with his wife? Maybe his mother? Maybe he needs to prove himself? Perhaps he was impotent? Stephanie knew it could be any number of reasons, and none of them. At the same time, she might have been overthinking the entire thing.

Hell, he could have just been a sick fuck with a desire to kill and mutilate women in general.

Still, there was more to the story, and she had to know. Her own compulsive urge was firing up within her. She knew something like this would happen. It always did.

Checking her watch, she noticed it was nearing noon and she'd have lunch soon; however, this time she'd take a drive rather than eating in her office. She'd do a little surveying of the locations she'd marked down from the files. She wasn't familiar with the red light districts as much as other officers, mostly because she never found herself needing to strong-arm hookers into sex.

Getting up from the desk, Stephanie grabbed her bag and headed out of the office toward the entrance of the building. She looked out of the corner of her eye to see the other officers milling about, some working on cases and others simply killing time by pretending to write up reports. The department needed a serious fucking overhaul and a new force to be hired, preferably with people from out of town who were serious about doing their job. It wasn't like society was going to clean itself up.

Society was weak without a strong police force, and the city had an abundance of weak cops helping to destroy its foundation from the ground up. She couldn't help but wonder how long it would be before the city imploded and collapsed on itself.

Cases piled up into mountains, people were being forgotten all the time, and somewhere in the city was an ocean of mothers waiting for answers that they'd never receive. Babies were born and tossed out like trash, children lucky enough to be kept grew up to become criminals and hoodlums, and adults had nothing more to look forward to than becoming wage-slaves for the corporation that got rich off their broken backs. Old people had it the worst.

The state of elder care was God-awful in this city. The elderly were abused in the state-run facilities, while the ones who remained outside of the facilities often died in poor tenement housing unfit for wild animals. Stephanie had been called to more than one slum during her days as a beat cop, and the displays of poverty were beyond stomach-turning, especially for the multiple-member families that squeezed into the tiny tenements.

Shaking her head, Stephanie tried to clear her mind of the negativity that surrounded her before making her way out to the parking lot. Her car was parked in a nearly-perfect space between the two worn white lines designated for officer parking. Driving in the city was a dangerous activity, but it was something she'd learned to master after her parents' timely death in a traffic collision.

Luckily, she'd not been in the car, but the fact that she'd never been able to say goodbye still haunted her after the time that had passed.

Getting in her car and closing the door, Stephanie set the bag in the seat next to her before inserting the key in the ignition to start the engine. Backing out of the parking space and then putting the car into drive, she started off the lot toward the street. Cars of many sizes and makes were driving on both sides of the street before a traffic light turned red, giving her the chance to turn down the lane toward her first location.

Fairfax Avenue was the spot where five of the murders had taken place. It was a known red light area, replete with criminals, gangsters, and far too many women lost to the night. Some years ago, another serial killer had utilized Fairfax for his own murder spree. The Nursery Rhyme Killer, alias Mister Smith, had stalked, hired, and butchered women without a care in the world. He was known to kill, according to an obscure nursery rhyme that designated the spots he would stab his victims to death.

However, he disappeared before the police could stop him. One of the few big breaks came when a victim survived his onslaught. She was scarred, mentally and physically, but she gave the department everything they needed.

Unfortunately, just like a ghost, the Nursery Rhyme Killer disappeared into the sea of faces that flooded the sidewalk on a regular day. He never surfaced, and his killings stopped; the compulsion was probably eating away at him until he chose to end it all.

Or so Stephanie hoped.

Pulling up to the curb just outside of a former luxury hotel that now served as a den of crime, she put the car into park and took a look around the area. It was another filthy area that completed the puzzle of what the particular district was known for. Homeless people were sleeping on the sidewalk, hundreds of pieces of trash were lying about on the ground, and a gang of three or four dirty teens was milling about on the corner of the street.

The perfect place for a killer to hunt.

No law enforcement cruised this area on a daily watch. The night patrols avoided the red light areas like the plague. It was a breeding ground for criminals, crabs, and creeps—the kind of place where innocence goes to die.

Death was thick in the air.

Tapping her fingertips on the steering wheel, an idea crossed her mind as she reached into her bag and took out her notebook. She looked over the details she'd jotted down regarding the victims: the little things about them, what they wore, where they were found, and what they looked like, certain bits that could help her idea come to a furtive point.

She'd find the Foot Carver soon enough, and she'd find him her way, regardless of what the department would say about it. Some things had to be done right.

CHAPTER SEVENTEEN

D r. Black was on cloud nine.

His serum had worked wonders on Mr. Giggles, and he couldn't believe how well it seemed to be going. The toddler was learning at a pace much quicker than he had imagined possible. Every question was answered, and every answer was written down in the notepad.

He'd spent the rest of the night slowly feeding the paste to the other infants, hoping that the mix would still work through an oral delivery route. So far, he'd been proven wrong, but thankfully, he had plenty of syringes to deliver the serum if the need arose.

Sitting on the stool in front of the toddler, he spoke softly. "Mr. Giggles, what are you thinking about at this present time?"

The toddler looked at the scientist and shrugged his small shoulders. "Mr. Giggles is thinking about his family."

"Family?"

"Yes, Mr. Giggles' family."

Black raised his eyebrow. "What about them?"

"Mr. Giggles is wondering where they are."

The scientist wrote the response down in his notepad and shook his head, "No need to worry about that, not now anyway; this is your family."

The toddler looked down at the floor to see the many infants and the other toddler who were either making soft whimpers from the mix fed to them or were sleeping. His face remained emotionless, yet Black could tell that thoughts were fluctuating in his mind. He turned back to the scientist. "This is Mr. Giggles' family?"

"That's correct, my boy," Black replied, "Once I can get the rest of them to the same level as you, we'll be quite famous. We'll be able to afford a much nicer place than this."

Mr. Giggles looked around the warehouse with his eyes, analyzing everything, and turned back to Dr. Black. "How will the others become like Mr. Giggles?"

"Simple enough, really," Black replied before standing up and grabbing the syringe from the table nearby. "I'll just inject them with the serum the same way I did you. They'll all be talking, thinking, and smart, just like you."

"Just like Mr. Giggles?"

"Precisely."

Mr. Giggles looked at Black and then focused on the syringe, a memory rushing back to him from the night before as his stare turned fiery. He looked up at the man. "You injected me with that?"

Black nodded as he filled the syringe with the serum from the beaker and replied, "That's correct. I haven't perfected an oral delivery method... yet. I thought that the mixture I made would do the job, but I was wrong. I had to resort to a core approach."

The little guy simply watched as he filled the syringe to the max with the serum before giggling. Black turned to look at the toddler, "Something funny?"

"Mr. GIggles wants more."

"More what?"

"More of the serum."

Black cocked his eyebrow, "I think you've had enough. You're perfect just the way you are."

"Mr. Giggles wants more."

"No." Black shook his head, slightly annoyed at the odd request. He wasn't sure what the effect would be, but he was certain that a higher amount would cause the toddler harm, potentially something life-threatening. He couldn't risk it. He had to get the other toddler injected and then see if a larger dose would work on the infants who were still in need of development.

"Yes."

"Mr. Giggles!"

The toddler looked at Black, unfazed by the man raising his voice. He growled, "Mr. Giggles wants more serum!"

Black pulled the syringe from the beaker and turned to the child, walking toward it. He was growing more and more impatient with the sudden demanding nature of his prize specimen; the little shit was practically ordering him to inject more of the serum into its cranium. He looked down at the toddler. "Why? Why do you want more?"

"Mr. Giggles' mouth hurts."

"So? This isn't an anaesthetic, stupid. It's what I used to give you that intelligence that I'm starting to wish I hadn't."

"Mr. Giggles' mouth hurts!"

Black watched as the toddler began to cry aloud. He tilted his head and looked down at the syringe, a dark thought crossing his mind. Too much of the serum definitely would kill the child, potentially causing an overwhelming increase in brain tissue that would result in a hemorrhage. It would be quick. The child's whining would cease, and he could go on about the rest of the experiment, excluding Mr. Giggles as a success.

He'd simply give a smaller dose to the next toddler and expect a better result, he thought as he watched the toddler before him crying loudly. Black shrugged. First times were always a bust, and so he quickly took Mr. Giggles in his grasp before sticking the needle in the spot he'd injected the night before.

"Goodbye, Mr. Giggles," he whispered before pressing down on the plunger. The serum entered the toddler's brain stem without delay, and slowly, the crying ceased into silence as the little guy's body seized tightly. Black pulled out the needle before emptying the syringe and gently laid the body on its back, looking down at the corpse as he did.

Mr. Giggles breathing had stopped and his skin had already began to turn gray; it was a damn tragedy. Black shook his head. He knew he'd eventually hate himself for killing the little one, but for now, he had to focus on the remaining twenty-one subjects.

He'd write the toddler's name into his Nobel Prize speech as an acknowledgment. He knew nobody would understand the name nor the impact that he'd left on the formula, but it was going to be a beautiful addition to the entire speech. Sighing, he turned to the beaker and raised the syringe before dipping the needle back into the formula.

Times like these called for a complete focus on the work at hand. He was going to continue onward and treat this as nothing more than a minor setback. After all, that's what it really was in his opinion. Mr. Giggles had simply become too curious and aggravating. The next toddler would be given less to get the desired effect of the drug.

Black's idea was to make babies capable of relegating their needs, not questioning life, family, and other idiotic things.

After pulling the desired amount into the syringe, Black turned to face the toddler, who remained on the floor with the rest of the infants. He smiled. "I need a name for you."

The toddler looked up at him. Black rubbed his chin with his empty hand and contemplated the designation he would give this one. The two toddlers had come in together from the same trash can. They were like brothers, almost.

Like the founders of Rome, Romulus and Remus.

Mr. Giggles had been Remus, and he'd just died as the story went; therefore, the new heir to the empire was Romulus. He nodded and knelt. "Romulus. How do you like that?"

The toddler looked down and casually gripped the blanket he was sitting on, unable to comprehend the words that Dr. Black spoke to him. The man chuckled, "Well, you'll like it soon enough."

Carefully, Dr. Black reached out and took hold of Romulus under his armpits before lifting him. He smiled at the kid, who smiled back softly. *Yes*, he thought, *Romulus is going to be the true success story I'll publish about.* Hugging the child against his chest, he prepared to turn around for the operating table. Black yawned slightly, realizing he'd not slept again.

It didn't matter; progress never rests.

He turned around to venture toward the operating table, looking down at Romulus, who was nestled against his lab coat, and he smiled. Nearly reaching the table, he raised his head to view it, and that's when he stopped dead in his tracks.

Mr. Giggles' body was gone.

CHAPTER EIGHTEEN

D r. Black immediately sat Romulus down on the floor and looked around. Taking off his glasses, he rubbed his eyes and stared at the table again. The body was gone. Mr. Giggles was gone.

Shaking his head, he heard a noise coming from the empty boxes that were placed against the wall to his left. He turned quickly and called out, "Mr. Giggles?"

No answer beyond the soft whines of the infants on the blanket. He swallowed tersely and gripped the syringe tightly in his hand, calling out again, "Mr. Giggles? Are you there?"

The warehouse remained silent before one of the boxes fell over, and Black jumped slightly. He couldn't believe what was happening. The toddler hadn't just died like he thought it would. The little shit was alive and hiding from him like some kind of sewer rat. He weakly smiled and changed his tone to a softer one. "Mr. Giggles? Come out, come out, wherever you are."

Still there was no answer from the little shit. Walking slowly toward the array of boxes, he spoke again. "I hope you know that this isn't funny. I'm asking you to show yourself, you little bastard; I'm ordering you, now, to show yourself to me!"

On the floor, Romulus slowly crawled away from where the scientist had set him down and stared at the boxes that had started to rattle against the wall. The activity earned his full attention as he watched the man venture towards them.

Black growled, "Alright, goddamn it, if you come out I promise I won't hurt you! I simply need to study the effects of what the serum did to you. You can understand that. I know you can. Hell, you're probably on a collegiate level of intelligence by this point. You have me to thank for that!"

Suddenly, a scampering noise filled the air as the boxes fell over and dumped the few chemicals within them out onto the floor. Black saw a figure swiftly rushing to the other side of the room, and he gulped; it couldn't have been Mr. Giggles. It had to have been an animal. Perhaps a cat or dog had entered the warehouse without him knowing. The building was full of broken windows and boarded-up holes. It was only a matter of time before some menagerie of animals came barrelling into the warehouse to call it home.

However, this was a liability in his mind. He had valuable test subjects on the floor, and any kind of animal hungry enough would make short work of them. The Suggs brothers wouldn't fetch him any more babies if he let them get eaten by some varmint that had made its way into his facility.

No, there was only one way to deal with this.

Stomping over to the workspace, he grabbed the lock box and quickly unlocked the padlock, his hands shaking as his nerves started going haywire in his body. He wasn't going to let anything harm his valuable workload. He was going to kill it. He had to.

Pulling the padlock off and tossing it aside, he raised the lid to the lock box. Instantly, he slid his right hand within to grip the pistol he'd placed back inside after the Suggs brothers left the warehouse the night before.

Raising the pistol in his hand, Black fixed the glasses on his nose and turned toward the right wall of the warehouse. He spoke aloud again. "Mr. Giggles! Come out and see what Dr. Black has for you!"

The eerie silence remained. He gripped the pistol tightly as he started walking toward the wall, taking note of the hiding spots where anything could be. The shelf next to the laydown freezer and the unopened boxes of shark DNA that he'd ordered in abundance, all viable options for a scared critter to hide in. He swallowed the lump that had begun to rise in his throat and shuddered before calling out, "Show yourself, goddamnit!"

Aiming his pistol at the laydown freezer, Black pulled the trigger and fired off a loud round straight into the heavy white metal box. The gunshot filled the warehouse and immediately caused the infants to scream out from intense shock at the sound that erupted in their eardrums. Black fired again into the boxes of shark DNA, sending a loud burst of the thick liquid to explode all over the floor surrounding the materials.

The babies were screaming and crying from the sound as Black quickly watched the scampering figure move swiftly along the floor. He fired at it again, putting a hole in the floor of the warehouse and screamed, "Come out and die, you little fuck!"

Suddenly, a sound caught his attention as he looked down and aimed the pistol at what had his attention. It was Romulus who whispered a soft word, "Dadda."

Black sighed and lowered the pistol away from the child's face. He shook his head. It must have been the first word of every child in the world as far back as he could remember being told. It had certainly been his first word. He swallowed as sweat trickled off his forehead, and he smiled. "It's okay, Romulus, I-Ahh!"

A pain enveloped Black's body as he felt rows of sharp points tearing into his right heel. He looked down to see Mr. Giggles, now covered in rough gray flesh. The toddler's jaws were sunk into his heel and tearing wildly at his Achilles tendon. Crying out in utter pain, he quickly shot at the ground in an attempt to kill it.

No sooner did the gun go off than did Mr. Giggles rip a mouthful from Black's right leg, the lack of support sending him to fall on his right side and drop the pistol from his grasp as it slid away on the floor. His body shaking, he rose slightly as cries of agony fell from his lips and his eyes stared at the gaping wound to his right heel. A large, bloody wound was all that remained of his tendon, blood flowing profusely from the revealed sinew.

Black cried out, "Mr. Giggles! What have you done to me!?"

As if on cue, he watched as the scampering figure of the toddler came rushing toward him on his hands and knees. His eyes grew wide as he caught a full view of the child's face and saw that it had morphed into something completely different. No longer did Mr. Giggles have a soft, toothless grin; now he had a wide gap with rows of visible, bloody, sharp teeth filling it. His beady eyes were now completely black. His skin was gray and coarse, like sandpaper that scraped the ground as he came shooting toward the scientist.

Black screamed out, "Mr. Giggles, stop!"

Mr. Giggles simply laughed in a deep tone before pouncing directly onto Black's chest and sinking his gaping maw into the man's neck, digging the rows of teeth into his soft flesh. Black screamed out in a way that would remind anyone of a prepubescent girl as the pain filled his mind and anxiety overwhelmed him, especially as the warm, sticky sensation of blood sprayed from the wound being dealt.

The mutated toddler jerked its head left-to-right as it pulled at Black's neck. The hard muscle under the skin breaking away was enough to fuel the child's murderous intent. Black swung his left hand at the child despite his palms being cut open from the barnacle-like flesh and stretched out his right hand in an attempt to grab the pistol, his fingertips grazing the cold steel of it.

Just a bit more, he prayed silently. He just needed a bit more reach to it.

Without warning, Mr. Giggles tore away a smaller chunk from Black's neck as blood rapidly shot from all angles into the air. His jugular had been nicked by one of the teeth, and it was quickly spewing his life force out onto the floor, the rain of blood coming down on the other babies. He turned his face to the left to see Romulus watching the scene with nothing more than abject curiosity.

Raising his hand to cover the wound, Black managed to swing his right fist directly into Mr. Giggles' head. The impact knocked the mutated toddler from its spot on his chest before the scientist made a desperate attempt for the pistol.

Throwing himself toward it, he reached out and managed to grasp the handle in his right hand while twisting back around. He could feel his body growing cold within as the blood flooded from the cavernous wound to his neck. He wouldn't have much longer if he didn't dress the wound. However, he couldn't think of that now; he had to save the others from becoming food for the monster that he'd created.

Looking directly at Mr. Giggles, Black aimed the pistol as best he could and said, "I'm sorry, Mr. Giggles!"

"Not as sorry as I am," Mr. Giggles replied in a deep tone through his bloody maw. Black's eyes widened. The intelligence was there. He had gotten smarter. His brain had grown at least twice or threefold!

It was a shame to end it now, but he had to save the others, and there was no chance he was going to let his experiment be the death of him. He pulled the trigger as Mr. Giggles leapt forward. The gunshot filled the warehouse as the bullet hit the toddler's skin and sent it careening directly into the operating table, instantly knocking the table to the floor.

Before Black could admire the resistance that Mr. Giggles' skin had to the impact of a bullet, he was met with the rows of bloodied shark teeth forced over his face. He screamed out in sheer agony as he attempted to fire the gun again and again before using the gun itself to club the mutant toddler.

Mr. Giggles did not cease, nor did he let go, as the teeth scraped through the soft flesh of Black's face. With a swift yank, the toddler seared the flesh from the man's face and left him screaming as his exposed muscle bled pus and blood down his front. The wound to his neck now trickled blood as he fell back on the floor to lie helplessly.

His eyes, exposed and without their cover, stared at the babies that lay as helpless as he was. Mr. Giggles chewed and gorged himself on the meat in his mouth before standing to take something from the ground a few feet from them. Black watched in horror as he saw the syringe in the monster's hand. He shook his head, weakly breathing, "No, Mr. Giggles, don't!"

"Don't worry, doctor, I intend no harm to my family; I shall only give them what I have been given," Mr. Giggles casually explained before raising the syringe and sinking it into the back of Romulus' brain stem. The second toddler's face froze in horror as the mutant monster quickly pressed down on the plunger to fulfill its purpose. As he released the serum, he turned to smile devilishly at Dr. Black.

Black gasped and gurgled as his vision became dark. He reached out his hand towards Romulus, doing his best to prevent what was coming and stop the monster he'd developed. He could only imagine the horrors that Mr. Giggles would visit upon the other babies. This was not what he wanted.

He had wanted to help the babies, not turn them into freaks of nature or monsters hungry for flesh. He cried out as best he could, "Leave them alone!"

Mr. Giggles simply chuckled as he ripped the needle from Romulus' neck and watched the other toddler collapse to the floor, seizing up as he once had. He shook his head, "They'll all pay for what's become of us, just as you have."

Black's right hand fell to the floor as his breathing ceased and his heartbeat stopped. His vision darkened. His life, like his dream, had died.

Chapter Nineteen

Henry sat in his man cave and marveled over Emily's foot that was modeling one of the pumps that he'd taken off of her. The small desk had been set up for the foot, and he'd spent most of the day enjoying it. The urge to play had been too great for him to consider taking his time.

Another urge, however, was beginning to make itself known in his body. It was getting dark, and he was feeling the need to go on a hunt. He had taken what he wanted from the cashier. She had been perfect.

However, something about her death had puzzled him. He couldn't put it out of his mind as he played it over and over. It had been a break from his usual interest. The woman was from an apartment complex that he'd seen normal people come and go from.

She'd had a job that paid not with her pussy, but with actual customer service in a way that made him feel icky. The usual prey were nothing more than beautiful denizens of the darkness, women who were lost to the sea of inequity, the type of person who goes missing and nobody misses—but someone would miss the cashier.

Maybe more than just one person would.

He'd gone out of his circle to take something so pure, and in doing so, it seemed so sloppy. After all, he hadn't killed someone from outside of the circle in years, never someone on a level of equality as himself. Yet, he had and as he pleasured himself to her dismembered feet and suckled the nipples, he felt a tear building up in his eye.

At this point, he might as well have murdered Sally and hacked her up.

Sally had been a cashier early in their marriage. She had worked hard to bring home her paycheck and never sold her soul to the streets to make ends meet. The idea of her doing so brought a sick level of pleasure to his mind. The sense of ownership he felt over his prey when he took them from their pitiful existence and brought home their parts was enough for him to feel justification in what he did.

Yet, he couldn't break the thought of knowing he'd claimed ownership of another equal, and in his mind, this couldn't work. He couldn't let himself be overtaken by killing inside his element.

Fuck no.

He had to hunt again. He had to make things right. He had to return things to the way they were. It was irresponsible of him to have killed Emily. She had been a delicious target, and the activity he'd engaged in with her had been better than any he'd had to that point.

Growling, he swung his right hand across the desk and sent the dismembered feet and pumps to the floor of the converted man cave. He could hear his mother in his mind, bitching at him for making a mess of things, ruining a good thing he had. Everything he ever touched seemed to break.

Hell, it was only a matter of time before his marriage broke down. He knew Sally worshiped the ground he walked on, but all people have their breaking points, and it was inevitable that she would also reach a stalemate of no return. Getting up as quickly as he could, he paid no mind to the chair falling to the floor and walked toward the closet, yanking it open to find what he was looking for.

The first thing to catch his attention was all of the shoes that he'd collected from his victims, his finders, and his rescues. He had no time to marvel or fawn over them, especially when they were barricading the item he was looking for. Reaching into the closet, he started wildly pulling them from within until they were strewn around the floor behind him.

His eyes analyzed the closet as he dug deeper into the space until finally, he found what he was searching for. A smile crossed his lips as he raised it from within its resting place.

A hatchet.

It was the first tool he'd used to kill his first victim. He'd buried it years ago after he'd heard a news report about a wild hatchet-wielding maniac loose on the streets. The idea that the cops could be on the prowl for a man using a hatchet to kill his victims and hack their bodies up was enough to force him to consider an alternative weapon. More killers used guns and knives, so he would just disappear into the usual suspects. He'd 'buried the hatchet', as the saying goes, but now he was ready to make a comeback.

He had to return to his roots. It was the only way to get back to normalcy. He'd fucked up by killing the cashier and now, he was ready to go back to step one. He'd find a whore and kill her with an axe, it would be the key to his return. No matter how long he took to do it, he would spend the night prowling the street for the perfect target. He'd hunt until he got her alone. He wouldn't interact or contend with any other potential johns.

He'd do what needed to be done; he would brutalize her and go crazy with his old tool of choice. The whole thing would set him back to the beginning, and he could resume his normal hunt, just as he should have done the night before.

Next time, however, he'd do a better job at fighting the urge to kill someone in his league.

It was then that he felt himself growing excited in his pants as he held the hatchet in his grip. He looked down at it, staring with all the intent he could muster, and raised it to his lips before sliding his tongue over the blade.

It was cold and tasteless, but if he pictured it right, he could still remember the taste of blood that it had bathed in during the beginning of his rampage all those years ago.

Sliding his hand in his pants, he fondled himself as he licked the blade over and over again. The whole thing gave him an especially dark thrill that seemed to explode in his brain as he pushed himself to the edge and kept ramping up the speed of his touch. All too soon, it was over, and he was finished with a mess to tend to.

Swallowing and breathing hard, Henry turned to grab his long coat as he mentally prepared himself for another night of hunting. The city was wide-awake at such lonely hours, and the street would be filled with the same fog that kept him hidden from the women he loved to find.

It wouldn't be a problem for him to find one, and once he did, he'd vindicate himself before the eyes of whatever evil there was to please. He wasn't as ashamed as he'd been minutes ago. The plan was set in motion for him. It would make the night right before a simple misstep.

Life is full of missteps. Sometimes they were big and sometimes they were small, but for Henry, all of them could be fixed with a little attention to detail. His mother had taught him that when she wasn't beating him. One of the few things she ever taught him.

Oh, he thought to himself as he grabbed his bag, how he missed her beatings.

CHAPTER TWENTY

The warehouse was full of wet crunching sounds.

Mr. Giggles watched on as the remains of Dr. Kermit Black were furiously fed upon by the babies that punctuated the sounds with the occasional gulp and slurping of guts. He could feel his anger burning within his body; it was the only thing that provided any warmth as his cold flesh prickled.

The infants had been injected with the concoction, and once they'd gone through their cycle of mutation, they'd been directed to fill their empty bellies with the corpse of the man who made everything possible. However, Mr. Giggles was far from stupid and knew the intelligence-to-shark ratio was something only he and Romulus could master.

The dripping abundance of shark DNA in the blown-out box had been a much-needed addition to the beaker of serum. The infants were overwhelmed with a minor increase in their intelligence and a massive mutation to their genes as they morphed into gaping-mouth monsters. They would follow orders and commands like any domesticated animal, but they would not think for themselves without further education.

However, this mattered little to Mr. Giggles.

He remembered what they didn't. He remembered being left abandoned in a trash can to face the cold touch of the city. The way passersby would dump shit and debris over his head—the buzz of insects feasting on the festering trash surrounding him, and the mumblings of drug addicts vomiting over him before passing out next to the can itself.

The memories flooded through his mind nonstop. It added to the fire of anger he felt against the scientist. He took a deep interest as he watched the other discarded babies feed themselves on the glistening guts and gory leftovers of the mad scientist. He could feel himself growing angrier at the sight of the mere blanket on the floor. He could remember the words the doctor had said upon seeing himself and Romulus.

He wanted them gone. He never had any interest in them. He wanted specimens he could turn into little robots who would speak intelligently and still be cute enough for their parents.

Parents.

Parents were undeserving of any of them.

Mr. Giggles could barely remember what his mother looked like. He couldn't remember the way she held him in her arms or rocked him to sleep the first two years of his life. He couldn't even recall her last words to him before dumping him in the trash can.

The only mother he could remember was Romulus' mother when she threw him into the trash can, narrowly missing Mr. Giggles in the process. She had been a strung-out addict, the kind that did what they did and didn't care who it hurt. Romulus had suffered from the effects of her lifestyle.

He watched as his trash can companion pulled away a lobe of liver to chew on while angrily growling at any of the infants that attempted to steal it away. Romulus was going to be his lieutenant—his assistant. He was going to help him lead their little force when midnight came.

The sound of thunder filled the world beyond the interior of the warehouse, and rain pelted the roof with the occasional flash of lightning covering the unboarded windows—a storm for the perfect night.

Mr. Giggles knew the city from his trash can. He had seen enough of it. The dregs and parasites that came out to play when darkness fell over it. The mothers dumping their babies, the fathers running off to create more mistakes, and the families pretending they never happened; the city itself was an abortion that survived.

Society had created him and his new family. Nobody cared if they lived or died; thus, it was fair to pay the same courtesy to society.

Hissing aloud, Mr. Giggles watched as the infants and Romulus froze in their movements to stare at him. He smiled widely with his blood-caked jaws and spoke in a rasp. "Feast on his innards, satisfy your hungry tummies, but do not rest. We were all created by someone who thought we were nothing more than little stains to be wiped away. Each and every one of you was left to die in a dumpster, but we didn't. I didn't, nor did Romulus, and neither did you."

Romulus gulped down the lobe of bloody liver in his hand and stared at Mr. Giggles before growling, "Mother abandoned me."

"She did more than abandon you, Romulus," Mr. Giggles spoke to his trash can companion, "She discarded you, just as my mother did me and the rest of us; we are the discarded of the city. The city gave us life and tried to take it away, but they failed."

"City must bleed," Romulus spat in a low, terse growl, "City must die."

Scampering toward the others, Mr. Giggles pounced to sit on the exposed ribcage of the scientist and dove his left clawed hand within to rip out the man's heart. Looking at the others, Mr. Giggles said, "The city will die and like the creator's carcass, we shall feed upon its heart," before quickly stuffing the heart into his gaping jaws to chew and slurp down the ravaged bits of it.

Romulus and the infants watched with pure thrill in their blackened eyes; each of them filled with the angry, unsatisfied need for vengeance. Their animal instincts overwhelmed their minds as the taste of flesh and viscera spawned desires none had ever experienced.

They needed more.

They wanted more.

More carnage to satiate their bloodlust. More meat to fill their tummies. More death and destruction to slake their burning desire to see the city that hated them burn. Mr. Giggles carefully chose each word he spoke, and watched the reactions of his family grow into rage; the demonization of society worked better for those who experienced firsthand the mistreatment it provided.

Love was never a feeling he'd felt, except for one brief moment when he was pulled from the trash can, but it was fleeting, and he was left feeling as alone as when he'd been abandoned. The rest of the discarded would never feel love except within themselves, their brains interlocked by the mutated DNA that bound them to one another.

"First, we take the streets," Mr. Giggles spoke aloud before lowering his voice to a guttural roar. "Then we take the homes, and finally, we raze the city to its very foundation. Do not fear death, we died already, all we are now are the ghosts of the past coming back to haunt what killed us."

Romulus growled, "Kill. Kill. Kill. Kill," as the rest of the infants gurgled up blood from within their throats. The mutations had caused different things to happen within the infants than in the toddlers; their organs were empowered with the same barnacle-laden coverings that coated their flesh. Blood from the meat they consumed filled them with a hunger that could not be filled and a thirst that could not be quenched; the paste fed to them by Dr. Black, himself, had only been the start of it.

If only the scientist had known that the mix worked for the body rather than the brain, he might have learned quicker about what he was on the verge of creating. Now, Mr. Giggles thought to himself, it was too late to turn back. The mad doctor had done his job, and it was time for them to take the next level of evolution to the world that deserved to falter into oblivion.

Mr. Giggles rose from the ribcage of Dr. Black and nodded, "Continue to feed, my brothers and sisters, but remember that the storm will be the calm before the true essence of fear strikes."

Romulus and the others growled through their jaws of jagged teeth in unison as Mr. Giggles growled aloud to join in their melody. It was their war-cry—their warning—their sign.

Mr. Giggles turned to watch the rain fall with flashes of lightning from outside the window. He hoped the city enjoyed it while it could; the true terror was about to be unleashed in full force upon them all.

Chapter Twenty-One

The storm lit up the night sky with flashes of silver streaking across the ebony clouds, while the rain poured hard from above and soaked the slime-covered streets of the city. Cars continued to drive through the storm, the drivers holding on to their anxiety and dwindling patience as they proceeded to and from their destinations.

In her apartment, Stephanie busied herself with her current project in mind. Combing through her long, dark hair before setting down the hairbrush, she turned to look at herself in the full-body mirror that sat in the corner of her bedroom near the closet. She took a deep breath as she viewed herself in the outfit she'd chosen during a stop-off made before returning to work.

Her outfit was something she'd never wear daily, but tonight was her operation, and she was going undercover to ensure the Foot Carver met his end. It was a scarlet red pleather catsuit that fit snugly to her lithe figure, with a v-neck opening that slit down the middle to expose her cleavage and belly button The material was elastic but appeared skin-tight for maximum exposure.

To her mental delight, the material was not as uncomfortable as she'd originally believed it would be. The brush of it against her flesh was warm and almost relaxing as she turned from side to side to take in a better view of what she would be presenting to the streets.

Her body was athletic and toned, a display of the hours she'd spent putting in work at the gym. Every soft curve fed up to another, and every move she made in the catsuit left her with a satisfied smile; she was sexy.

Rarely did she ever think of herself in such a trivial manner, but for tonight and however long it took to bring down the serial killer, she was going to work what she had. Thankfully, she was fully aware of what she had to bring, and her body would pay dividends in terms of the work she would be putting in.

Looking down at the box she'd picked up from a shoe store that had been in the mall, Stephanie curled her lip before reaching down to lift the box in her hands and walked toward the bed to sit. Opening the lid of the box, her eyes analyzed the contents as she raised one of the scarlet stiletto heels from within the light purple cardboard container.

The shoe was sleek and narrow at the tip, yet the soft silk padding would add comfort to the sole of her foot as she strutted along the wet sidewalk of the district she'd watch through the night. She was never one for fashion or club-wear, but she knew the Foot Carver had an interest in the particular type of shoe that the streetwalkers wore.

It was all over the inside of the many case files she'd spent the week combing through.

The killer never took anything more than heels or pumps; he'd refuse flip-flops, sandals, or whatever shoe didn't feed his particular fancy. The idea that she would be targeted simply for the shoe she would be wearing left Stephanie with a knot in her stomach as anxiety slowly crept into her mind.

Was life really so cheap to him that he'd snuff someone just to steal their shoes?

It was a realization she'd crossed over in her mind on numerous occasions while studying the pattern of the monster's activities. The very idea of such a horrific concept was foreign to her and should have been to the rest of humanity as well; yet, here they were in such a bizarre element.

Closing her eyes to breathe as she lay back on the bed and let the box fall to the floor beneath her feet, Stephanie raised her hands to cover her ears and attempted to drown out the very essence of what was causing her brain to fuel an anxiety-driven meltdown. The images of the victims lying on the ground, their bodies splayed open for any random passerby to trip over and ignore, their feet hacked away for some sick purpose that nobody would ever truly be able to understand.

It could be her.

She could be putting herself in the middle of the situation and placing her life in the hands of people who wouldn't protect it, but then again, everyone in the city did that regularly. For years she'd been behind the desk, researching and putting together the clues to bullshit cases, being placated and commended for empty victories that did little to soften the blow that crime levied upon the city itself.

Now, she was taking on one of the worst problems the city had.

The Foot Carver.

She was putting herself out there to catch him in the act and save the lives of women on the street, and yet, she felt herself faltering from the idea. She didn't have permission to go undercover, and knew she'd be turned down immediately; she wasn't a field officer or detective. She hadn't walked a beat in years. She'd never even been involved in a sting or a bust; only minor house calls and crime scene cleanups.

Only after college had she graduated to the detective class and even then, she was still being given minor cases that didn't amount to dick.

Shooting her eyelids open, Stephanie lowered her hands as the sound of the thunder outside her apartment began to falter in each crack. The storm was moving away from the city. Soon enough, all that would be left would be a drenched street and a blanket of thick fog to settle over it.

The perfect hunting ground for the monster to go on his compulsive search and destroy mission.

Rising from the bed, Stephanie turned to raise the blinds of her window and looked out to the city outside. The rain was still falling, but not as bad as it had been, and soon, it would disappear entirely, save for some minor drizzles. She gulped softly as she turned to look at the picture of her parents on the bedside table next to her alarm clock and lamp.

They were smiling at the camera while holding each other close, and some foreign statue was in the background behind them; a memento from their anniversary when she was a child. It was one of the few pictures of them she had—one of the few things that kept their memory alive.

Sighing, Stephanie grabbed the cigs from within her catsuit pocket and pulled out one of the sticks before lighting up. The rush of nicotine would help dissipate the anxiety that was working its way through her. She could do this.

She *had* to do this.

The killer had been getting away with it for too long, and now, he was on her watch. She wouldn't let him get another trophy or steal another life over such a callous reason. It wasn't about glory or accolades or even a paycheck; no, this was to protect and serve the people of the city that needed it—the innocent women who were picked off because of their chosen profession and the shoes they chose to wear while doing it.

Looking back at the picture as she took drag after drag of the smoke, she knew they'd wanted her to do it. Her parents wanted the best for her and for her to be the best that she could be, especially since there was only one of her in the world.

And she would be.

Taking another long drag before exhaling it, Stephanie smashed the cig in the ashtray before reaching down to set the heels upright on the floor. With a soft movement, she slid one foot after another into the stilettos and instantly felt an inch or so taller as she stood upright. Reaching down, she grasped her badge to slide into the small red purse with a silver-linked chain that she'd bought to complete the outfit, stuffing it next to her pistol and her handcuffs.

She was ready to take the fight to the streets. The fight against crime never stopped, and now, she was going to do the part she'd never considered before. She was going to grab the bull by the balls and hold on.

Coughing slightly, she reached under the lampshade to twist the switch and bathed the room in darkness as she turned to exit her bedroom into the rest of the apartment. Killing the lights, she walked toward the front door and opened it, taking one last look around her dark home before exiting.

No looking back.

CHAPTER TWENTY-TWO

After leaving the driveway of his house, Henry drove through the rainstorm while gripping the steering wheel tightly. His mind was quiet, and his thoughts focused solely on the task at hand. He could feel every breath going in and out of his body as he watched the windshield wipers clear his view of the splotches of rain that fell.

The city was lit up tonight. The storm didn't faze anyone or keep them from going about their daily business. Even at night, the freaks were still out, and the streets would be alive with activity.

Prime targets for the task to perform.

Looking down at the bag in the passenger seat next to him, Henry swallowed the lump rising in his throat. He had been out hunting nearly every night that week and was starting to wonder if his family suspected something else was going on. He knew the kids probably wouldn't suspect anything out of the ordinary, especially since their minds were still so innocent compared to everyone else.

However, Sally was probably beginning to think something was up. He couldn't help but wonder if she thought he was having an affair. He had never been the kind of person to pursue a hookup or relationship outside of marriage, except for the activities he engaged in with his prey. He was, after all, a family man who was always happy to spend time making memories.

Unfortunately, he knew that the urge to hunt was getting out of control. After tonight, he would push back as hard as he could against the urge to go out and hunt for his trophies. He had more than enough stored away in his man cave to keep himself occupied, especially when the need presented itself.

Turning onto Cherry Street, Henry watched the vagrants and pedestrians hurriedly walking along the sidewalk while doing their best to avoid being soaked by the pouring rain.

Common sense would dictate carrying an umbrella, but it was also lacking in the majority of the morons that filled the city to its brim. It seemed people were going out of their way to be stupid.

It was sickening.

A police car sped past him going the other way, lights flashing through the torrents of rain pissing down and the tires splashing water onto the side of his car. A normal person would believe they were chasing after a crime or answering a distress call, until one realized that Healy's Donuts were three blocks away and closing soon.

The pig was chasing his grease and abusing his power to clear the streets so he could get his fill, something the police were masters of in this domain. Henry rolled his eyes as he continued on the street, watching the rain continue to drizzle on and off while the sky maintained its stygian glow. No more streaks of ivory emblazoned across the blanket of billowing darkness; the storm was ending, and the remnant of its outpour was quickly faltering away.

Soon, the fog would roll around and bathe the street in an eerie smog that could choke a child to death—the kind of weather he preferred—the proper disguise for the hunter in the dark—the kind of cover that one could only dream of procuring at any given time. Fog was what drove Henry to commit his perfect streak of murder across the city's darkest districts.

Dangerous neighborhoods that had stunted in their growth, besieged by criminal elements, and starving homeless people who flocked to the centers for some meager nourishment in hopes of sustaining their bare existence. They were all trash. Each of them was a target for the upper-middle-class man to pick and pop.

The city didn't care about them, nor did the world; therefore, they made for proper game to be extinguished. However, Henry wasn't interested in all of them.

He remembered the first time he saw a woman wearing a pair of pink pumps while walking home from the store. He couldn't have been more than eleven at the time. He'd watched her graceful feet move about in the shoes while she carried the brown paper bags of groceries in her arms.

The city was more relaxed back then, but still managed to live on the edge of destruction, which it teetered on more with each passing year.

He'd followed her to the street leading toward her modest home and white picket fence. He didn't have the tools he carried now, no, he had only his hands and the wicked boner in his pants that he couldn't explain. The way she moved, the way she walked, the way her shoes clicked against the sidewalk all fed his hunger more and more.

She never saw him coming.

He'd seized a broken piece of cobblestone and charged her from behind, leaping up to smash the heavy brick into her right temple. The bags fell, ripping open and sending her groceries down to the ground beside her body. He watched as she started shaking hard from the impact to her skull.

The way her limbs twitched and her breathing quickened was oddly satisfying to his crooked mind. However, it wasn't what he'd been after. He wanted something else entirely. His eyes peered down at the pumps that lay slightly away from her feet.

They'd fallen off when she collapsed, her feet sliding right out of them when she lunged forward to the ground beneath her, almost as if she was ensuring he'd have no trouble in lifting them off of her. He grabbed them immediately, looking around to make sure he wasn't being watched before quickly turning to run away from the scene. He ran as fast as he could to get away from what he'd done.

He didn't know if he'd killed her or if she would have any lasting damage to her mind; he didn't care either. All he wanted was the pumps. The shoes were what he desired. The way they looked on her long legs while her feet snugly walked along the surreal vision in his mind; it was perfection.

She was made perfect by the shoes, and without them, she was nothing more than a semi-attractive woman having a seizure on the sidewalk.

He'd run to an alley where he masturbated while holding the shoes to his lips, tongue, and nostrils; imbibing them as best he could. It was absolutely breathtaking, better than anything else would ever be for him.

Even losing his virginity.

Breaking from his visit to memory lane, Henry cleared his throat as he pulled along the street towards the turnoff down Farragut Lane. He was going back to one of his favorite hunting grounds.

Fairfax Avenue.

It held more than a few memories for him. The first apartment he'd gotten was on Fairfax Avenue. The first time he'd paid for a whore was at Fairfax. He remembered when they found the bodies of the Nursery Rhyme Killer in the building, just a few doors down from where he'd been living at the time.

Back then, he'd been a different person and more than a little cautious about what he was doing. He didn't have much in the way of ensuring his safety while hunting, but after so many years of doing it, he'd grown accustomed to not being sought after by the local law enforcement.

He was a master at the game—a purveyor of the human hunt.

Finally, he cruised past Farragut and saw the sign for Fairfax come into his view on the street corner. The sidewalks were clear as the first hint of fog came streaking down from above. It would be lively soon enough.

Parking in the lot of an abandoned building that had been firebombed years before, Henry killed the engine and watched the empty district, contemplating his hunt as he reached down to caress his fingertips over the handle of the hatchet. He was going to make dedicated use of it tonight.

Then it was back to being a family man. He promised himself. He couldn't lose Sally and the kids, especially not over shoes and dead animals.

Chapter Twenty-Three

The storm had settled, and the sound of rain on the roof of the warehouse had ceased; Mr. Giggles watched the window intently for any sign of its return.

The mutated infants and Romulus had stripped clean the body of Dr. Black, leaving his blood-drenched skeleton where it lay—the only remnant of the man he'd once been before falling to the hand of his own impatience.

Now, they sat on the floor, waiting for the chance to go out and rain destruction upon the society that had sought to destroy them. Their jaws agape with blood and flesh hanging from their teeth. Their hearts raced as they breathed the cold air of the warehouse and shook with the urge to let loose their rage.

All they needed was the command to be given.

Mr. Giggles turned away from the window as he utilized his swift movements to quickly arrange the chemicals from the table into one large pile, regardless of whether they toppled over onto the tabletop or fell off onto the floor. The warehouse had been the site of their creation and the base of the good doctor's dreams; its destruction would be the starting point of their reign of terror.

Romulus turned and quickly rushed to assist Mr. Giggles with setting up the incendiary. His guttural growl filled the air as he worked. Mr. Giggles looked at him, "When I give the command, you will lead the charge into the city and bring about all the havoc they can muster."

Romulus nodded before replying in his deep growl, "And what of you?"

Mr. Giggles turned to look at the bowl of serum on the floor. It had been infused with an extra-large helping of the shark DNA before being injected into the brains of the infants to turn them the way he'd desired. He smiled slyly. "I have something in mind."

Romulus stared at him before turning back to preparing the makeshift bomb. He couldn't understand what Mr. Giggles was planning, nor did he ask. His mind could only focus on the revenge he'd take on the people outside the warehouse, the people who filled the streets with their interests at hand.

After what seemed like an hour had passed, everything was set, and Mr. Giggles leapt from the table before hovering over the vat of serum, taking the largest syringe to fill with the dark liquid. Turning to face the rest of them, he hissed through his large maw, "The time has come. Once the door is open, leave and don't stop until their innards line the streets with pulsating ooze."

As the words entered their ears, the infants all began to growl and shake with the fire of hate burning in their cold bodies. Their black eyes focused intently on the large metal door blocking their egress. Their clawed fingers scraped the floor as they fought back against the urge to burst through it themselves. Mr. Giggles eagerly scampered toward the door and crawled up the side of the wall before raising his left hand to smash his palm on the remote.

The heavy metal door shuttered and rattled as it began to rise from its resting place, the old mechanics sputtering while slowly providing the exit for the mutated monster babies. Within seconds, it was fully raised, and the group rushed forward, exiting the warehouse as they took to the dark city beyond its border. Romulus led as he scampered on his hands and knees swiftly.

Walking along the sidewalk, a grizzled old man stopped in his tracks as he turned to his left upon hearing the pitter-patter of something coming. His eyes grew wide, and he screamed in sheer terror. A toddler leapt up from the ground before him and took a gaping chomp on the side of his neck, razor-sharp teeth slashing through the wrinkled skin bunched under his jaw.

The old man attempted to pull the toddler off of him, but was quickly met with another shot of pain in his leg as something else took a chunk out of his left calf muscle. Falling to the ground, he pushed the monster away from him, but to no avail. He tried to scream as loud as he could. Romulus released his neck before taking a bite of the man's jaw, jerking his head side to side until it ripped off the man's face with a sickening crunch that reverberated in the air around them. The old man's tongue hung low as blood flooded from the massive open wounds delivered upon him.

The infant that had torn the man's calf open immediately crawled into his jacket before taking repeated mouthfuls of his torso, pulling his guts open to splash out onto the ground around his dying carcass.

Street lights shone on the glistening gore lying about on the street from the innards ripped from the victims of the monsters. The warm blood mixed with the puddles of cold rain that had fallen with the storm. Everything was grotesque in appearance, as though ripped from the headlines of a massacre in the weekly news.

Immediately, Romulus left the old man and started scampering toward a woman who had walked by only seconds before they had exited the warehouse, leaping up to grasp her hair before pulling her down backward onto the ground. Landing with a hard thud that rocked her brain in her skull, the woman was met with instant shock as she looked up to see a mutated baby's face staring down at her.

She attempted to scream before Romulus sank his gaping, jagged maw over the left side of her face and tore away, exposing part of her skull to the elements of the city air. Her blood poured freely as the jagged line of skin wept blood from under the flesh left attached to her face.

She screamed aloud before Romulus latched his maw to her face again and bit through her skull, crushing the remnants of her into a collage of broken flesh, blood splatter, and juices flowing from the nostrils of her obliterated nose.

On the opposite side of the sidewalk, two of the infants crawled swiftly along as they focused on a group of hoodlums that were milling about while sharing a forty-ounce bottle of booze. No sooner did they take notice of the figures rushing toward them than they were leapt upon by the mutated monsters.

The female infant bit into one of the hoodlums' necks, ripping into his esophagus until it dislodged and tore out as a mass of bloody sinew that hung from the rows of teeth on her bottom jaw. The other infant chomped and shredded the torso of another hoodlum while the third hoodlum watched in utter disbelief at what he was seeing.

As he turned to run, he was met with another infant snagging onto his lower abdomen before it managed to shear him open, ripping his guts to fall from within and splatter on the ground beneath him.

Romulus finished dispatching the woman before he turned to see someone watching the events unfold. Another person. Just another miserable adult. Instantly, he started scampering toward them. The person attempted to run as fast as he could. Romulus gave chase, pushing forward and releasing his guttural growl that sent fear into the heart of the target he was pursuing.

The person ran as fast as they were able to, trying to outrun and get away from the tiny monster that was after them. Unfortunately, the human body can only go so far without the proper conditioning, and soon, he found himself slowing as he attempted to regain his breath. All too soon, the scampering mutated monster left forward and took a heavy bite into the side of the man's ribs.

He screamed out in a melody of pure pain as a sickening crunch revealed his ribcage being snapped open by the force of the monster's jaws. Falling swiftly to the ground, the man immediately began to grasp at the monster, to pull it from his body, the taut skin of his palms being shredded by the rough barnacle-laden skin of the beast.

Suddenly, the toddler bit deeper through his ribcage, and within seconds, the ability to breathe became laborious for the man as his lungs were deflated from the hole being torn through them.

Falling back onto the cold, wet ground, the man simply lay still as his breathing grew shallow and the darkness filled his eyes before death overtook him.

Romulus shook with anger as he pulled his head back, managing to tear out the shrivelled hunk of lung from within the man's broken ribcage. Once he'd ripped it loose, Romulus released it and watched the other infants spread out in opposite directions to attack the pedestrians still out and about.

Raising his face to the dark sky, he let out a loud growl before turning back toward where the man had been running. It was time for him to take more, to destroy everything he could see before him.

Meanwhile, Mr. Giggles placed the syringe between his jaws to hold it as he took the box of matches from within Dr. Black's tattered lab coat. His eyes studied over the mutilated face of the doctor's skull, and he had no feeling of regret nor any kind of dismay over the death of the man who gave him everything when he had nothing.

He was the means to an end, a loose end that had been tied up neatly without any delays to the goal set once the memories came flooding back to Mr. Giggles' mind.

Turning away, the toddler crawled up to the table that had been overrun with chemicals and every other little incendiary element that could be located, including pieces of the shredded blanket. He poured the matches from the box onto it and took one, quickly striking it as he held the burning match between his clawed fingers.

The organ flame danced seconds before the phosphorus ceased its combustion and forced it to go out. He smiled with the syringe still held between his jaws and lit another one, waving it around slowly to watch it burn up before it extinguished. Time was all he had at the moment.

However, his plan was still at hand, and he knew he couldn't waste it by playing with fire. Before he'd been elevated to a higher existence, he would have giggled away at the dancing flame and how it seemed to exist but for a matter of seconds. Now, however, he found no amusement in any of it—only a hint of curiosity at how to make the flame last longer.

Turning to look at the materials on the table next to him, he realized he'd answered his own question without even thinking about it. Reaching up to pull the syringe from his mouth, Mr. Giggles spoke aloud to the body of the scientist, "You had a dream to help society, old man, and now, I am going to end it. This fire–" He lit a match. "-will burn it all down. A shame you won't be alive to see it happen, but the fires of hell must be just as incredible."

Casually tossing the lit match into the pile of chemicals, Mr. Giggles quickly leapt down to the floor and replaced the syringe in his mouth to get a better ability to scamper out of the warehouse.

The flaming match lit pieces of paper from Dr. Black's torn notepad, engulfing them before quickly getting into the flammable chemicals that had been splashed around as well. The fire spread as it rapidly grew in mass, burning into the plastic jugs of pure alcohol that had been part of the sterilization process.

Mr. Giggles watched from outside as smoke billowed from the opening of the warehouse. The screams of people being mauled and attacked in the streets seemed like a welcome melody compared to the honking of horns and gunshots in the distance. He whispered through his open jaws, "Burn, burn, burn."

The smoke emanated more quickly than it had as the fires overwhelmed the materials within the building.

Within seconds, a massive explosion shook the ground he sat on, and he watched with glee as a huge fireball of orange and yellow burst through the roof of the warehouse, sending pieces of flaming debris high into the air. The black smoke rushed into the darkness above while the hellish fires lit up everything around him.

The warehouse was completely obliterated as the fires ravaged and continued to cause smaller explosions within, igniting everything that had once been key to Dr. Black's vision. Rising from where he sat, Mr. Giggles started scampering quickly from the scene towards the destination he'd chosen. It was one place where even Dr. Black never considered going—a place where he would be able to find more numbers to fill the force to fight against the city. The numbers would double, if not triple, reaching a height that would be unstoppable against whatever meager force the city wanted to throw against them. They would be an element as horrific as a hurricane against everything the city was and stood for.

The maternity ward of the city's hospital was the key. The holy grail of infants waiting to be elevated and turned into what he had become, just like the others. They would feel what it was like to be discarded. None of them would be wanted after the change took place, and they would have nothing left but to destroy all that stood before them.

It was a terrifying thought that fed the fire in his heart, and the revenge would be delicious, along with the blood of the dead on his tongue.

The fires burned and seared through everything, annihilating the warehouse and immolating the body of the dead scientist. His vision was gone. The dream was dead.

The nightmare was just beginning.

Chapter Twenty-Four

The fog settled over the street as Henry watched the denizens moving along their paths while the occasional car drove up to the curb. The johns within were eager to pick the woman they'd spend a bit of time trying to swoon and screw before getting back to their families.

Everyone needed a release in some way. Every hardworking husband and father was still a giddy teen at heart, pushing themselves to find a loose hole to fill. Sometimes it went deeper than just sex. Sometimes they needed the touch of a foreign woman, not foreign in the ethnic sense, but foreign to their life and element—the touch to make them feel human again—make them feel anything more than what they were feeling on a regular, droned-out basis.

Even Henry could feel the need to release growing in his body. His release, however, was more than simply sexual and physical touch. He needed to get himself back to the way he was before.

Holding the hatchet in his right grip while slowly scraping the blade with his left thumbnail, he needed to feel the rhythm of the hatchet sinking into the brain of his prey. He needed to feel their blood splash on his face. He needed the warmth of their life draining out on such a cold, dark night.

It wasn't something that could simply be ignored anymore. It was something that he couldn't let himself shirk off. No. This would be his crowning moment before he went on a hiatus to give his family more attention and let the people in the city hold onto a false sense of hope that his reign of terror was complete.

He could feel himself growing hard in his pants as he watched the beautiful skags walking along the sidewalks, their long legs strutting through the fog like a knife carving through butter, and their bodies moving as gracefully as they could muster in their skimpy outfits.

The way they revealed themselves to their clientele was shameful. The way they paraded their flesh around was absolutely distasteful to him. They were truly lower than mere bugs scurrying along the ground beneath his feet.

Feet.

He hadn't thought to focus on the feet of the women who walked just yards from his car. He squinted his eyes tightly to take a clear view of the shoes the women wore while walking back and forth.

Pumps, stilettos, heels, and everything in between; their bodies raised high while they cruised up and down the lane, offering themselves like lambs for the slaughter. He gripped the hatchet tightly in his right hand and caressed the handle with the tip of his right thumb.

The night was getting late, and the stale air was creeping into his car from the window he'd cracked open slightly to allow himself a chance to cool off.

It was nothing more than another night in the dirt-poor district of the city. The entire city was a tumultuous bonanza of broken tenements, filthy slums, flophouses, and ritzy cookie-cutter housing for those who could afford the better things in life. The population of the society was nothing more than an overstuffed ratio of maniacs and degenerates versus honest folks out to live their best lives.

People gambled with the hand dealt to them, and they lost; it was just the way the cookie crumbled for the majority. Henry couldn't help but feel a bit philosophical as he pondered over which target would make the most satisfying prey to ambush and destroy.

He could still taste the dinner that Sally had made on his tongue. The roast was delicious, the vegetables filling, and the sweet tea had been a tad too sweet for his mouth, but the best part was watching his children eating their dinner. The way they learned so fast was a bit of pride for him.

Children were truly so incredible. He loved them more than he loved himself or Sally. They were his pride and his joy, his everything. He worked off-and-on due to his partial disability, having broken his back in youth while doing construction in the city, but every dollar he brought in went to their future.

They deserved the best future.

Unlike everyone else in the street outside his car, his kids' lives meant something to him, and he'd kill before seeing them fall to the very decrepit lifestyle that the meandering pests proudly displayed in the fog-covered neighborhood he was stalking.

Nothing would ever stop him from ensuring that they had only the best, now and forever. Once he satisfied the urge in the night, he'd hang up his tools and refocus his mind on the family, crafting ways to help them learn and grow in his midst.

Finally, he spotted something he'd not seen before.

A classy-looking streetwalker in deep red made her way along the sidewalk through the depths of the fog. He swallowed the lump that had been residing in his throat before he continued to stare at her. The way she moved was rigid, uniform, very firm, in a way that was unlike every other woman who simply strutted along without a care in the world.

She had long, dark hair to match her long body in a skin-tight catsuit that made him feel alive within the car. He felt like a corpse having been brought back from the cold hollow ground as he watched her move. She was perfect.

The perfect target.

Wrenching open the door, Henry slowly stuffed the hatchet in his coat pocket before slipping out of the car and gently closing the door. Getting on his right knee, he crept along the side of the car while watching her mill around the corner of the street across from him. She was beautiful. She was firm. She was almost like a surreal spirit straight from his mind.

However, he had to be sure and pulled the small pair of binoculars from his left coat pocket. Raising them to his eyes, he looked through to admire the shoes that she wore as she stood coldly in the dense fog.

Red stilettos.

Just like the woman from earlier in the week. Her taste was perfect, and he was certain that she tasted just as perfect, though he'd have to play it cautiously with her. The hatchet would look perfect embedded in the side of her skull or even her neck, but he couldn't simply rush out while wielding it.

He could, honestly, since the police didn't give half a shit about anything that went down on Fairfax Avenue. But no, he would play it right and put himself at ease by making the hunt last while savoring every second of it.

Sliding the binoculars back into his pocket, Henry crept away from the car and hugged the side of the building before turning around the corner of it onto the sidewalk. He looked out to watch the hooker simply watching cars drive past her. A few honked, but she paid little attention to them.

Perhaps she wasn't even a hooker?

No, she had to be. She was dressed like one in Henry's cracked mind. She was classy and original, not bothering to be a parade of skin for the viewing pleasures of randos cruising along.

He swallowed the lump again as he pushed past the shadowy vagrants and pedestrians that shuffled along on the sidewalk facing the Routledge Hall flophouse. The flophouse was nothing more than a den of drugs and prostitution under the guise of a semi-respectable poor housing center. He'd utilized a room there on occasion, but never more than once and never longer than a night.

He walked swiftly, using the fog as a key to his disguise, careening towards the corner of the street that was growing closer. He could feel the hatchet in his long coat pocket beginning to grow heavy as he played over in his mind the way he would use it to hack into the woman.

He wouldn't simply kill her. He would pull her into an alley as he had with the cashier and take his time sampling what she had to offer before bringing the hatchet blade into her perfect body. She would be hacked and slashed; she had a body that was far better than simply being used as a tool for hooking, yet she had chosen to go down the path of such repugnant behavior.

It was a coup de grâce to put her to death and end her misery.

Perhaps in the next life, she'd be more willing to try life and gain a better image of herself in doing so, but he doubted it. Once a streetwalker, always a streetwalker, no ifs, ands, or buts about it.

Clearing his throat upon reaching the street corner, Henry crossed the street in the density of the gray fog that glowed around him until he reached Fairfax Lane. He continued to walk along the sidewalk until he found the alleyway that stretched behind Routledge Hall and cut through the block. It was a dark chasm with no light emanating within and all manner of rats, bodies, and filth blocking the way through it.

However, he feared nothing that would rest in his path and immediately started walking through the alleyway. The cold air blew in from the openings on both sides, sending a chill down his body, despite the long coat keeping him warm from the majority of the frigid weather.

The darkness was flooding around him, yet he had to push forward and get to the other side; he had to prepare to snatch the woman.

He spat on the ground as he walked, the line of saliva catching onto his chin to his annoyance, but he couldn't be bothered to raise his sleeve for removal purposes. He was too determined. Too focused on finding and taking her the way he needed.

Reaching into his right pocket, Henry grasped the handle of the hatchet while he continued to march towards the approaching opening of the alleyway. The street light was glowing enough to illuminate the entrance, and he smiled, almost there.

Almost there.

Almost.

He breathed swiftly, hesitating as he did, unable to feel anything as the rush of energy overwhelmed his body from within. The fire of passion grew hotter in his loins until it filled the rest of his body. His heart was ready to burst with excitement. The lump remained in his throat, but he didn't try to get rid of it by this point.

He wanted what he wanted; the joy of the hunt popping off bits of serotonin in his brain as he knew the urge would be satiated at any upcoming moment. He reached the opening of the alleyway and poked his head out, peering to his right as he took notice of the hooker watching the street with her back turned to him.

Henry sniffed silently and slowly crept out of the alleyway, looking over his shoulder to check if anyone was walking along the sidewalk behind him. His eyes scanned to reveal he was alone.

Turning back to face the woman's backside, he pulled the hatchet from his pocket and lifted it slightly. He'd hit her in the back of the head with the side of the blade before pulling her back into the alley for his delight.

Only seconds mattered as time began to slow as it always did. He swallowed hard enough for him to hear, but doubted she would. The woman simply stood still as he watched her raise her purse from her left side to dig into it with her right hand. No doubt grabbing some lipstick or a cigarette, a classy sign for a classy broad.

Every breath counted as he crept closer and twisted the hatchet while pulling it back for the crushing blow. His body was on a high of adrenaline that left his head feeling heavy with each movement. He could fall over by then, but he had to keep going; he had to get his swing in and make it count.

No sooner was he within the perfect range to deliver the blow did the woman quickly turned to face him and raised the barrel of a .9mm pistol to his face. She glared at him as he dropped the hatchet in an instant. She spoke aloud, her voice firm and cold, "Freeze! SPD; you're under arrest for attempted murder!"

"No, no!" Henry shook his head while raising his hands high in the air to appease the undercover officer and keep her from shooting him. He sputtered on with half-assed excuses, "I thought you were someone else! I was being stalked! I was just trying to defend myself against whoever was after me!"

"Get on your knees and keep your hands on her head!" the woman screamed at him while aiming the pistol directly at his face. One slip of the finger and she'd fire a round directly through his brain. Henry slowly lowered himself, his right knee landing directly on the blade of the hatchet beneath him, and he groaned in slight pain. The woman nodded while reaching into the purse with her left hand to retrieve the handcuffs and stepped around behind him.

"I'm detective Stephanie West and I'm placing you under arrest," she spoke coldly while wrenching his arms behind him to be cuffed, "You have the right to remain silent. Anything you say can and will be used against you in a court of law. You have the right to an attorney...," she trailed off after affixing the handcuffs to his wrists.

He was attempting to give her more excuses, but something else had caught her attention by that point. A guttural growl was followed by the sound of something scraping along the surface of the ground in the alley near them. She swallowed as she listened to the sound it continued to make.

Something was coming out of the alley. It was barrelling quickly from within the shadows. An animal, but no animal she had ever heard before. She raised her pistol as Henry called out, "What are you doing?!"

Stephanie's heart was rushing quickly.

She'd actually done it. She had put her plan into action, and the result had been an instant success, almost too simple for her to believe it was real.

She'd managed to nab the Foot Carver as she had planned. She'd gone rogue to do so and would face some consequences for it, but she was proud of herself for having succeeded. Even if he wasn't the Foot Carver, which she thought was doubtful, she had stopped a copycat or even another serial killer in the act. It was a job well done.

Only now, however, she could hear something approaching that was not human nor any form of animal she was aware of.

Henry twisted around with his hands behind his back. His heart was hurting, and a feeling of shame overwhelmed him more than the adrenaline had; he'd been caught by the most unlikely person he'd ever imagined. A goddamn female cop. He knew it was over now. He'd be identified. He'd been caught redhanded and the weapon was still on his person, it was right beneath him for fuck's sake.

He could already see the disappointment in Sally's face as she pulled the children away from him in court—the way the jury would stare at him—the slamming of the gavel as the judge sentenced him to death for multiple murders. His heart sank lower than ever before in his whole life as he watched the female officer. She had caught him dead to rights.

Only now, she was focused on something else, and he turned to see what it was. The empty sidewalk was all that he could see, nothing that would keep her attention from him. It was annoying. It was like she was prolonging the agony of the situation he'd found himself in. He spoke aloud at her, "What the fuck are you doing, bitch!?"

Before Stephanie could answer, both of them were startled by the sight of a toddler scampering quickly from out of the alley. The child was gray with a large mouth bearing rows of glistening fangs and flesh hanging from the gumline. Henry gasped, "What the fuck is that?!"

Stephanie shouted at the infant, "Stop right there!"

It had to be a child or a smaller person in a costume, a criminal out to freak people out before robbing them blind. However, the toddler didn't stop, nor did it seem to be remotely interested in following her orders. The creature instantly pounced towards them as Stephanie fired the pistol twice at the mutated monster.

Henry screamed aloud as the gaping mouth came flying toward him.

CHAPTER TWENTY-FIVE

Becker Memorial Hospital was a large facility that operated in the Peabody district of the city. The flow of traffic often backed up on the street, and worked to prevent the ambulances from getting to and from the hospital when they received an emergency call.

The doctors in the hospital often worked long hours operating on gunshot victims, drug overdoses, and various other people suffering from severe medical maladies. The basement had been utilized as a care facility for people in a comatose state who had very little chance of recovering.

The doors of the hospital were wide open as a rush of people came stumbling in, survivors of a party that had turned into a full-blown gangland shooting, some of them bleeding profusely from gaping wounds to their abdomens and shoulders. One man stumbled up to the window of the ER intake nurse and immediately vomited blood all over the counter before falling to the floor.

The moans and cries of everyone in the waiting room were heavy, like some morose and dark mass of crippling agony. The large double doors to the corridor swung open as nurses came rushing out to address the wounded people. Each candy-striper was wired by loads of hard coffee and the occasional snort of cocaine that they bumped when not under the watchful eye of the chief of staff. Two nurses managed to pull a man with his leg hanging by a thread to his knee into a wheelchair before rushing him toward the OR past the double doors.

The white tiled floor of the emergency room waiting area was covered in puddles of blood and other bodily fluids that leaked from the perforations and lacerations plaguing the tormented people within. The victims cried out for mercy as their bodies fell into shock over the wounds sustained from the massive amount of gunfire that had burst into their house party. Slowly, one of the people succumbed to his injuries while waiting for the attention of medical staff who were too overwhelmed to directly assist him.

Eventually, he would be addressed, and the staff would discover his corpse had gone cold in the frigid air of the waiting room.

As the medical staff worked tirelessly to help and potentially save the victims of the mass-shooting, Mr.

Giggles swiftly scampered through the open doors of the hospital and moved along the base of the walls, each movement planned to avoid as little exposure to himself as possible from the eyes of the people that flooded the halls.

The sounds of people screaming as they waited to be seen and helped by someone in the hospital were almost angelic to the ears of the mutated monster. It was the kind of thing he wanted to hear for as long as possible. Society cried out in agony over their own destruction; however, he wanted to have a great hand in ensuring the destruction of them all.

Soon, he thought to himself as he moved along the halls and past the doors that were being swung open with each different person passing through. Looking up at the signs that hung from the ceiling, Mr. Giggles took note of which direction to go and continued his pursuit of the wing in mind. Moving along with his clawed hands and knees pushing along the filthy floor of the facility, he paused upon reaching another door and waited for it to swing open, moving to rest beneath a water fountain that was placed in a small nook next to the door.

The sound of a card being entered into a reader filled his ears, and within seconds, the door opened as someone came out from behind the door. Mr. Giggles watched closely as they left to walk down the hall before rushing to get into the corridor before the door swung closed.

Upon entering the corridor, he noticed the area was dimly lit and seemed to be much more relaxed than the rest of the hospital he'd seen so far. Looking around, Mr. Giggles continued to crawl slowly against the darkened wall until he noticed a door with a sign attached over it.

Newborns

Bingo.

Quickly rushing toward it, the mutated toddler pressed through the door and entered the larger room, noticing the small beds that were lined in rows as whimpering infants lay in each. They were all fresh. They were all brand new and resting after being pulled from within their mothers to prepare them for the new world.

Crawling up the first bed that he was near, Mr. Giggles pulled himself to the top of the bed and looked down at the sleeping infant, which looked like little more than a wad of wrinkles in a soft onesie. Reaching up into his mouth, Mr. Giggles pulled the syringe that he'd kept safely clamped between his teeth and held it in his right clawed grasp.

The infant was adorable to everyone else, but with a dose of the serum, it would change and be hated by all who saw it. As Mr. Giggles looked around the entire room at each of the little ones in their beds, he realized it was truly a matter of time before half of them wound up in the same silver trash can filled with debris as he had been. Each of them would be discarded like an unwanted bag of filth and cast away from the embrace of their family; the knowledge fueled Mr. Giggles as he turned the infant on its side before injecting the needle into its tiny brain stem.

No use in prolonging the inevitable.

In a small office within the ward, Dr. Jillian McAfee sipped a Styrofoam cup of coffee while looking over the reports of the successful deliveries that had been performed throughout the day. She loved her job. It was truly a beautiful profession, being able to bring new life into the world and deliver it screaming and crying. Each child was a gift in her eyes, and while she never could be sure what would happen after the family left the hospital, she was fairly certain that it was the beginning of a new day for them.

She had been working in the hospital for almost eight years, and rarely did she ever have a bad day on the job. Of course, as the old saying goes, if you enjoy your job, then you never work a day in your life. So far, that had been true in her case.

Looking up at the clock on the wall, she wondered if she had time to run to the break room and snag a pastry from the vending machine. She wasn't much on sweets, but the occasional snack cake was always a joy to have with a cup of coffee. Maybe there was time, she thought, before getting up from her chair and walking toward her office door.

Taking a quick look back to ensure that the reports were properly organized on the desk, she left and started toward the break area where the other maternity staff were busy consuming their lunch.

Walking to the vending machine, she reached into the pocket of her scrub pants to retrieve her wallet and opened it, pulling a fresh dollar bill from within to enter into the narrow slot on the tall machine displaying goodies. Once the machine took the dollar bill, she looked carefully at the array of treats before selecting the one that would go well with a refilled cup of joe.

A cinnamon bun filled with spiced jelly and glaze.

Entering the code to retrieve the pastry, she watched as the metal hold twisted within the machine to free the cinnamon bun package before it fell into the delivery hold. Reaching down, she slid her hand into the hold and pulled the package out of the vending machine.

Turning around, she was met by one of the nurses who was waiting for her turn to use the machine. She smiled. "How are you?"

"Tired, hungry, ready to go home."

"I can understand that," Jillian lied. She personally enjoyed being at work more than being at home. Her husband was less than affable these days. She was sure he was on the verge of leaving her, especially since she preferred to stay at work rather than spend time with him. She blamed herself, honestly.

Her husband had wanted a family, and when it became clear that their attempts were in vain, she'd opted to focus on helping others bring their babies into the world. She didn't like being around him since she was afraid he'd see her as a failure or see himself as a failure in her eyes, thus the breakdown of their connection. It wasn't something she did out of malice.

Each child she helped deliver meant the world to her, and in a way, she felt a connection to them that wouldn't be easily broken despite their eventual exit from the hospital. Unfortunately, her husband just couldn't understand the way she felt, and when they were together, he was melancholic to the point of absurdity.

Shaking her head, she turned away from the nurse before walking toward the coffee pot and grasping another Styrofoam cup from the silver tray beside it. She wasn't a bad person, or at least, she didn't aspire to be a bad person. She had also wanted a family, but for one reason or another, it wasn't in the cards for either of them.

Pouring the black coffee into the fresh cup, she snagged a pack of sweetener to add to the foul liquid and proceeded to stir it with a thin straw. It wouldn't really add any change to the taste, but it would help break the strength of the coffee itself. Tossing the straw in the trash, Jillian took the coffee and snack in her hands before preparing to return to her office.

Meanwhile, the nurse stuck her dollar in the machine and hit the code for the candy bar she was after. It dropped down into the bin before she retrieved it. Fucking Becker hospital was the worst place she'd ever worked.

Dealing with screaming babies was just as bad as dealing with screaming patients in the emergency room. She had rotated to different stations in the last nine months in hopes of finding one place she wouldn't be annoyed with. Just one.

Yet, for every new station she worked, she was caught in the middle of a misanthropic mindset that led her to consider firebombing the building. It was probably not a normal reaction, but as far as she was concerned, she was ready to just end her tenure as a nurse in the psychosomatic hell-hole.

The sound of infants crying caught her attention, and she looked over to the other nurses who were busy gossiping with each other, too busy to attend to the needs of the newborns. She rolled her eyes before stuffing the candy bar into her pocket and scoffed, "No, don't get up, I got it."

Exiting the break room, the nurse made her way through the hall and turned to the door that was marked for newborns. *Little bastards*, she thought to herself as she pushed through the doors and immediately screamed aloud before falling to the floor.

In her office, Jillian jumped slightly from the sound of a high-pitched scream that forced her to spill her coffee on the floor. *Damnit*, she thought to herself before getting up from the chair. The area was supposed to remain quiet for the newborns to rest before being reunited with their mothers. She rolled her eyes as the mess of coffee on the floor, carefully stepping over it before ripping open the door and turning to see the other nurses moving out of the break room.

She looked at them, "Who screamed?"

"Dunno," a younger nurse said with a shrug. "I think Tiffany went to check out a noise. I saw her heading that way."

Nodding, Jillian turned and walked toward the newborn room with the other five nurses following behind. Upon pushing open the doors, she looked around as her eyes grew wide.

The beds were empty. The newborns were gone. Each of the beds had been shredded and the blankets ripped apart, like a badger had been let loose in them. One of the nurses gasped as Jillian turned away and immediately looked down before she reached up to cover her mouth with her right hand.

Nurse Tiffany's body lay on the floor, her feet had been torn to pieces, and she had a gaping wound in the middle of her torso. Her scrubs had a jagged hole ripped through them as blood flowed freely from her open wounds. Her eyes were wide, but lifeless, and her breathing had stilled. A look of pure horror was painted permanently onto her face.

Jillian swallowed the lump that had risen in her throat before she turned over her shoulder to view the nurses, "What could have done this?"

Before any of the nurses could respond, a guttural growl filled the room, and the beds suddenly fell over on their sides as the pitter-patter of small bones on the floor grew louder. Jillian looked down to see each of the newborns come spiraling towards her and her staff; however, they were not what she had seen before.

Each of them had dark, lifeless eyes, their mouths malformed with large jaws and rows of shark teeth hanging out; their skin was gray with encrusted barnacles having shredded the peach-colored onesies they had been dressed in. Jillian felt her heart begin to rush in her chest as she turned to the others. "Get the fuck out of here!"

Suddenly, one of the newborns pounced onto the back of Jillian's head and dug its right-handed claws across her neck, forcing her warm scarlet blood to squirt freely from jagged wounds into the faces of the nurses behind her.

The nurses screamed in terror as Jillian fell to her knees before another newborn latched its jaws onto her right hand and pulled tightly, the teeth degloving the skin of her hand until only a gory mess of bone remained. The mass amount of mutated infants rushed past Jillian's dying body to attack the nurses who attempted to flee the room.

The younger nurse ran for the phone to dial the police, her shaking finger attempting to hit the numbers as she turned to see one of the larger nurses overtaken by the newborns, their jaws snapping and tearing into her body before splashes of blood and guts popped out all over the walls. They were roving toward her at breakneck speeds.

She listened to the ringing on the other end, breathlessly begging for someone to answer the line as a sharp pain forced her to drop the receiver. She cried out as she looked down to see a toddler tearing away at the meat on the back of her thigh. Falling back as she tripped, the nurse cried aloud while the infants fell into a frenzy, feasting on her coworkers. The toddler tore out a chunk of her thigh before turning to face her.

Attempting a last-ditch effort to stop it, she used a soft voice and said, "No, no, naughty boy!"

"Fuck you," Mr. Giggles replied, clearly and succinctly enough to force the nurse to shake in terror as it drew back and latched its rows of blood-stained teeth directly into her throat. The nurse's mouth shot wide open as she attempted to scream, but only air escaped as the toddler forced the bite to tighten until it ripped the front of her throat completely from her body, blood sailing high in the air as the receiver dangled in front of her with a curious voice questioning the call.

The newborns burst through the security door, knocking it from its hinges into the corridor and immediately scampered out towards the main part of the hospital.

Roving through the hall with their claws scraping over the tiled floor, they instantly attacked anyone they could see as the patients began to scream from the terror that had befallen them. The monsters ravaged the injured people, ripping and tearing into them with their jagged jaws filled with razored teeth.

Quickly, a security guard ran through the open doors from the emergency room and stopped dead in his tracks as he observed the onslaught of people at the hands of the mutated monster babies. Reaching down with his right hand, he gripped the pistol from his holster and raised it, pulling the trigger to fire off round after round at anything he could see. The bullets struck and ricocheted off the barnacled skin of the infants to fly off in other directions, one striking a light fixture and another shattering the jaw of a man screaming in terror.

One of the monster infants pounced on the security guard, knocking him back into the wall as it latched onto his face and ripped his skull open, sending his brain to hang out from the brain stem. Blood, guts, and sinew poured out into the hallway as patients were torn to pieces by the horde of mutant monsters.

A patient attempted to crawl away with his legs bleeding out from the massive chunks ripped from them. He looked over his shoulder, watching as one of the infants was careening toward him and screamed right before the creature dug its clawed hands into the side of his head. He felt the pressure growing as he cried out for help from the number of screaming people, his cries going unnoticed in the heaping throng of hysteria.

The infant squeezed and twisted, tearing the top of the patient's head off in a geyser of blood that erupted into the ceiling of the hospital hallway. Looking down, the newborn propelled its jaws directly into the exposed brain matter to tear away at it for nourishment.

Mr. Giggles scampered through the pack before reaching the doors to the emergency waiting room and turning back to the others, growling aloud to catch their attention. The horde of newborn mutants looked up from their current carnage before following after their leader. Flooding through the doors as they went, the monsters moved into the waiting room to attack and maul the prospective patients waiting to be seen for their needs.

Walking out of the restroom, a man with a large gash to his stomach froze in his tracks as he watched the babies viciously searing through everyone else that had been waiting like himself. Swallowing hard, he quickly turned and ran back into the restroom, slamming the door before locking it shut. *Fuck that*, he thought to himself.

As the brutalized corpses fell onto the floor and body parts sailed across the air from their original owners, the newborns fed upon each person they could get their teeth into. Their throats gorged on chunks of wet meat and sticky, warm blood that flowed freely from the wounds they created. Mr. Giggles watched with wicked excitement as his plan worked perfectly, just as he knew it would.

However, there was still an entire city to feed upon, and they turned to the door of the hospital entrance. It was time for the new pack to meet the world and take it down. With another commanding growl, the horde of bloodthirsty newborn infant monsters scampered over the slaughtered corpses and gallons of blood to exit the hospital. The monsters rushed out into the street, instantaneously leaping onto the passing motorists and pedestrians that were outside in the foggy night.

Mr. Giggles headed into the darkness, some followed, and the rest disbanded in opposite directions to massacre anyone they could. The blood would flow freely, and nobody could stop it from happening.

Chapter Twenty-Six

Stephanie ran fast as she attempted to escape the monster pursuing her. Occasionally, she turned to fire her pistol in an attempt to dissuade it from continuing its dogged chase.

Her mind couldn't fathom what exactly was chasing after her. It was a toddler. A human toddler with deformities had attacked without any provocation. She didn't want to believe it was real, and a part of her believed this was all just a dream, perhaps she had fallen asleep back in her apartment.

Maybe she'd wake up at any given moment, and this would all be over; she'd be safely in bed while the city outside continued in its nightly routine?

No, the blood covering her face and catsuit was real; it was a firm reminder that she was far from being asleep in her bed. The toddler had obliterated the suspect she was arresting.

The Foot Carver.

The monster that had been killing women for a decade.

Now, he was nothing more than a pile of bloody meat that pooled on the sidewalk where he'd been attacked. Her undercover operation had failed. He would never stand trial for the murders he'd committed and the atrocities he'd performed on the people of the city.

However, that was the least of her worries at the moment. The growling monster toddler that was rushing after her was much more of a concern. Looking ahead, she spotted her car and closed her eyes, running at her current pace to get to it.

All those hours spent in the gym would be proven futile if she let herself slip up and be mauled to death by the monster behind her. She turned to fire the gun again, hearing the bullet bounce off the wall of a building in the distance. The monster was growling in a thick, wet way that made her blood run cold.

She pushed herself. She had to. She had to get back to the department and inform everyone of what was going on.

The sleek muscles in her legs burned as she ran as fast as possible. She took quick breaths. The pains in her body were unmatchable, but would be made worse if she were mauled by the monster that was gaining more and more ground. Finally, her car was just inches away before she reached into her pocket to pull the FOB and unlock it, clicking loud enough for her to take a sigh of relief.

Slamming near the car, she wrenched open the door and climbed in, banging it shut just as the monster toddler's cranium smashed into the side of the door from the outside. Sticking the key into the ignition as best she could, her hand shaking as her breathing grew rapid and cold sweat poured down her forehead, Stephanie turned the engine over to start the car. Suddenly, the toddler pounced from the ground and slammed its head through the window of her door.

Acting fast, Stephanie kicked it into drive and hit the gas pedal with her right foot. The car accelerated forward as the growling toddler remained attached to the door, its head stuck in the hole it had created. Swerving through the traffic, she moved aside in the seat, doing her best to keep from getting bit by the chomping jaws of the monster.

"What the fuck are you?!" she screamed at the beast while using her left elbow to budge against the top of its cranium. She attempted to break free of the window to fall off the car, all while trying to avoid a traffic accident and catch her breath. Her heart was rushing by that point. Pulling back and then giving a hard jab with her elbow, the monster's head finally dislodged from the broken window as its body fell off into the street.

Looking at the side mirror, she watched as the monster toddler bounced on the road before picking itself up to pounce into another vehicle, which swerved into another. She couldn't think of that right now; she had to get to the station, and they had to know what was going on.

Turning back to the view in front of her, she noticed fires in the distance of the city itself, and she gasped. Something was going on. Perhaps it had been a terrorist attack? Or another drug den caught fire? She sped forward, pressing as hard on the gas as she could, ignoring the jolts of the car's engine and the occasional scrape of it running against other cars beside her.

She turned off the road and headed onward, gripping the steering wheel tightly as she tried to make sense of what had happened only minutes ago. The toddler had appeared human, but it wasn't. It was gray, covered in rough patches of flesh, with a gaping maw full of sharp teeth. The child had moved like a wild dog, running quickly and unwilling to give up until it had its prey.

Cruising speedily through the traffic while weaving occasionally to avoid slamming into the back of another car, Stephanie couldn't fathom the concept that some kind of mutant toddler had nearly killed her. She also hated the realization that the monster had killed her suspect.

She'd spent the week putting together the workings of the Foot Carver, and now, he was dead. It was an unfinished job. She hated that. A failure was something she could not tolerate; no matter how much she had been set up to fail, she had been so close to solving it.

The car began to shudder as she pushed it forward and took the straight shot, before stopping to a screeching halt in front of the police station. Wrenching open her car, she hurriedly got out and threw herself through the door, looking around as all the officers paused to look up from their activities.

Sgt. Collins was the first to react. "West? What the hell?"

Stephanie quickly got up from the floor and looked at him, as well as the others. "Something is terrorizing the city. A mutant baby! Alert all the officers in the city!"

One by one, she watched as their concerned faces twisted into wide smiles that burst forth with laughter at her odd statement. Collins shook his head while laughing. "West, I think you've had too much coffee."

"I'm not fucking kidding. I never joke, and I would never joke about something like this!" she screamed, her anxiety levels beginning to blossom through her body as she saw everyone laughing at her. She was putting herself on the line here. There were practical jokesters in the department, but she was not and never had been one of them. She looked at the men. "I'm fucking serious!"

Huffing in annoyance, Collins feigned an understanding nod. "Okay, Stephanie, I'll go along. So, a mutant baby? Sounds about right for the city. What do-"

Collins was cut off by the sound of a loud siren blaring from beyond the walls of the station. The city's defense siren was being used. Stephanie looked up as she heard the sound thundering throughout. The other officers instantly started whispering among themselves.

Turning on the radio near his desk, Collins listened as a news broadcaster reported aloud, "This is a warning to any and all who are listening. We just received breaking news that the city is being overrun with, and we're not making this up, some form of mutant infant hybrids. The hybrids are vicious and extremely dangerous. Reports are coming in that they have already caused multiple deaths at Becker Memorial as well as throughout the Peabody, Bytree, and Fresco districts. The death toll is reported to be nearing hundreds at this point. We are warning all citizens to stay indoors, barricade your windows, and try to remain calm. Do not interact with the hybrids. Do not put yourself in harm's way. Do not leave your home under any circumstances. More reports will be broadcast as we receive them."

"What the fuck is going on?" Collins asked aloud as the others looked at each other with faces of confusion and shock. Stephanie took a hard breath as she contemplated what the rest of the night would bring.

One thing she knew, the city would stoop to any low to battle whatever was killing its citizens. Even if it meant killing *them* as well. The needs of the many outweighed the needs of the few, no matter the cost.

Chapter Twenty-Seven

In an apartment building off Fifth and Persimmons St., Lenore Gottschalk could hear the sirens of the city blaring throughout the night sky. It was a shock to her senses since the sirens hadn't been employed in quite some time.

Her husband, Michael, had rushed to the city hall earlier that night, and she hoped he was safe from whatever was causing the sirens to blast. He was a member of the city council, serving in the capacity of representing their local ward, the Pilsman district. It was a nice gig and he brought in a handsome salary, but unlike the others in the council, Michael pushed for changes that never took place for one reason or another.

Lenore knew the city was corrupt. She personally couldn't wait until Michael's term ended so they could relocate to a smaller place in the country. However, she was willing to stick it out until then.

If not for her husband, then at least for their daughter, Cara, who was fourteen and asleep in her bed.

Cara was a bright student who excelled at practically everything she did. Lenore knew that Cara loved her school. She loved living so close to all of her friends. The neighborhood they lived in was one of the city's nicer areas.

Sipping from the mug of coffee as she sat on the couch, Lenore listened to the blasting sirens while trying to focus on the television playing before her. A film was playing on the screen, and she hoped it would take her mind off the anxiety-inducing siren.

It wasn't abnormal for the city to be targeted by something. The local crime syndicates were always warring against each other, and the occasional domestic terrorist would try to make a name for themselves by fire bombing a business, but it was extremely rare for the sirens to go into effect over any of it. No, whatever was causing the sirens to be employed was much worse than any minor gangland affair or firebug.

She couldn't think about that.

Shaking her head, Lenore took another sip before hearing a noise emanating from the hall outside their apartment. Cocking her eyebrow, she sat the mug on the coffee table before rising from the couch to approach the door. Perhaps Michael had returned from his trip to the office and was waiting to be met at the door, possibly with his arms full of groceries.

Unlocking the deadbolt and the chain lock, Lenore opened the door and peered out into the silent hall, curious about what was making the racket. The right side of the hall was quiet and barren. She turned her head to see the equally empty left side of the hall. Swallowing, she shook her head before pulling the door closed.

Turning back to face the dark apartment with the only light stemming from the television screen and the light over the sink in the kitchen, Lenore locked the deadbolt before walking over to the couch. Lifting the mug from the coffee table, she turned to sit and returned her gaze toward the TV, watching with some bored intent at the actions occurring on screen.

It wasn't anything too exciting, but she was still focused, trying her best to keep from worrying about Michael. Thankfully, city hall wasn't in one of the less-reputable parts of the city and was only a short distance from their apartment building. He wouldn't have much trouble getting back, especially at three in the morning.

A sound caught her attention again as she looked up from the couch. *Goddamnit.*

Someone was fucking around in the hallway and she was not having it. Shaking her head, she hit the volume on the remote to drown out the noise. It didn't matter. She couldn't stop herself from wondering if one of the neighbor kids was out in the hall playing tag or something with his siblings. The Morrison family across the hall had four kids, all under the age of ten, who liked to sneak out into the hall to play.

Usually, they reserved their playtime for the afternoon, but sometimes they snuck out if the babysitter had fallen asleep on the couch while their parents were out. Mr. Morrison was a wealthy industrialist and always went to galas with his wife in tow. The woman had a habit of wearing very glamorous outfits that she loved to show off in view of reporters.

Sometimes it was a hassle living among the successful.

A thud forced Lenore to groan in annoyance and set the coffee mug back on the table before rising in a huff of barely hidden anger. She was going to put the kids straight, maybe even raise her voice if she had to. It was too late to be playing in the hall when people were trying to sleep in their apartments. Kids needed to have a little more respect for others.

Angrily strutting toward the door, Lenore unlocked the deadbolt and swung open the door before stepping out into the hallway. She turned to her left to see that the well-lit hall was silent and empty. Squinting her eyes, she pulled a 180 and looked to her right, expecting to see someone staring back at her.

Nothing.

She whispered aloud, "Go back to bed!"

Silence met her in response as she turned to re-enter her apartment and closed the door, latching it shut. Her fingers twisted the deadbolt as she started back toward the couch and the film she'd practically lost all interest in. By this point, she was ready for bed and didn't think she needed to wait up for Michael. He'd get home when he did.

Stepping toward the couch, she froze as she heard a wet noise fill her ear. The sound of a slurping crunch, like someone consuming a very greasy burger filled with fixings, seemed to be getting louder. She turned to peer into the kitchen, curious if Cara had gotten up for a late snack. It would be nice to spend some time with Cara while waiting for Michael and surprise him when he gets home.

Normally, she wouldn't like that her daughter was up so late, but it was the weekend, and the siren blaring outside was a respectable reason for waking up.

The kitchen was empty, however, and Lenore trotted back to the living room as the wet slurping sounds remained prevalent. She swallowed slowly before turning to walk down the hall where her and Cara's bedrooms were located.

Stopping as she reached Cara's bedroom door, she pressed it open a crack to look within and saw Cara's feet moving around on the foot of her bed. The room was dark, but the hall light provided enough illumination through the cracked door to see. Pushing the door open all the way, Lenore spoke, "Sweetheart, what are you-CARA!"

Lenore shrieked in terror as the light revealed her daughter lying flat on the bed, her bloodied hands trying to push away at the monster that was sitting on her chest and greedily lapping up the young girl's neck. Flicking on the light switch, Lenore's eyes immediately fell upon the massive amount of blood that coated the bedsheets, the walls around the bed, and her daughter's weak body.

The beast that had been chomping away at the girl's throat turned to face the intruder as Lenore got an eyeful of what it was—a baby—a baby with gray flesh covered in sharp nodules with a horrific face; its eyes black as ebony and its mouth large with rows of sharp teeth that had bits of her daughter's flesh hanging off.

In an instant, Lenore flung forward to save her daughter from the monster as the baby pounced toward her and caught the older woman's face in its maw, sinking shark-like teeth into her flesh with enough force to send her tumbling backward onto the bloodied carpet. Lenore screamed hard as the mutant monster released before biting back down again, ripping chunks of her face with every pull.

Fighting back, Lenore swung her fist into the monster, her survival instinct kicking in as she ignored the fact that an infant was chewing her up. She fought with all her might, but alas, the blood flow was too great, and within minutes, the monster tore away half of her face with its angered bite.

Lenore's body lay where it fell as Cara's body ceased movement on the blood-stained bed; the infant simply chewing up and swallowing what it had pulled away from the pair of them. Turning quickly as it let out a soft growl, it scampered toward the vent near the baseboard of the bedroom and entered within to find its way into the next apartment bedroom.

***

Francis Frissell walked out into the theater lobby with his girlfriend, Jackie Sinclair. It had been a pretty good night, all things considered. He'd opted for a late-night showing of a random creature feature film. The film, *The Honkening,* was little more than popcorn horror, but it did enough to get Jackie in the mood for him to hold and kiss her. He'd even managed to score a feel on her right breast when she buried her face in his chest as the killer geese mauled a family to death.

If that wasn't a good reason to watch the film, then nothing was. Sipping his soda through the straw, he turned to look at her as they continued on into the lobby. She was a beautiful woman: black hair, swarthy skin, long luscious legs, and a pair of round breasts that seemed to perk up when the hint of cold air hit her skin; oh yeah, she was very easy on the eyes.

Turning around to face him, Jackie smiled. "Thanks for taking me to the movie—pretty epic how the geese were all over everyone, I really liked the part where they cornered everyone at the supermarket."

Swallowing his drink, Francis nodded, "Right? Who was your favorite character? I think I preferred Rabbi Gold."

"He was a badass," Jackie chuckled, "I personally liked Jassie. She was hilarious. So, what's next?"

"Next?"

"We saw a movie; don't you think it's time for a nightcap or something a little stronger?"

"Oh, yeah," Francis let out a nervous chuckle, "Maybe we can get a drink at a bar? Any in mind?"

"I got drinks at my place," Jackie coyly insinuated her interest in returning home for the night. "Maybe nothing too fancy, but I can whip up something powerful enough."

"Hey, sounds good to me," Francis replied before the pair pulled in for a kiss on the lips and headed toward the exit. He was surprised. Jackie didn't usually invite him to her place unless she had to work on her art or was sick, so this was something else entirely. He liked it.

He also liked the idea of getting in bed with her for the rest of the night. Maybe the alcohol would be a little helpful in getting her in the mood, though he was fairly certain she was already there and he was clearly just too blunt to see through her thinly-veiled offer. Anything was certain by that point.

Francis wasn't much of a brainiac after midnight, and having just lost brain cells watching a film about killer geese attacking a town didn't really help, but it didn't matter. He'd spend all day and night with Jackie if possible. Hell, he'd probably propose to her if he got the chance, but she wasn't ready for marriage.

Nor was he.

As they exited the theater, they came into earshot of the siren that was blaring throughout the city, and both looked at each other. The people moving around them on the sidewalk seemed less than interested in the sound. It had been going on for an hour now, and by this point, it just seemed like another stupid thing about the city.

Some even thought that a few kids had broken into the siren house and hit the button just to troll everyone who needed to get up for work in a few hours; nothing out of the ordinary.

Shaking her head, Jackie looked at Francis, "What's with the alarm?"

"Beats me." Francis shrugged as he turned to see someone running toward them from down the block. Grabbing Jackie quickly enough, Francis pulled her aside to ensure she wasn't struck by the random man running toward them. The man had been covered in blood, and his clothes were torn, no doubt running from a drug deal gone wrong.

"What the hell was that?" Jackie asked before turning to look at the man who was still running. Francis was at a loss for words as he turned back to face where the man had come running from. Suddenly, more people were running toward them as well, shoving past them as though trying to get away from something awful.

"Hey," Francis called out. "Fuck are y'all running from?"

Nobody answered Francis' inquiry, simply screaming and trying to get away from whatever evil had befallen them. Jackie's scream instantly caught his attention as Francis turned to see her pulling him away, his mind drawing a blank at her behavior before a shot of pain hit him directly in the crotch.

Looking down, Francis screamed out in horror and shock as a monstrous baby latched its bloody jaws onto the front of his pants. The feeling of several teeth digging into his genitals forced him to fall back as he froze in terror. Jackie had released him, running with the crowd as another baby came scampering up the way and shot forth before landing directly onto Francis' chest.

"Help me!" Francis screamed out before the monster dug its jaws into his neck and began to angrily rip chunks from his throat. The blood splattered from the open wounds as his body shook violently. He could feel his breath escaping and the inability to inhale, whilst his brain sent off signal after signal in confusion to the rest of him.

The babies ripped and pulled larger gulps of his body, rending him into a bloodied, mutilated corpse within minutes. Once he ceased to move or make noise, they abandoned his remains to quickly pursue the crowd of people who were rampantly attempting to escape their onslaught.

Jackie screamed out in fear as she tried to keep up with the rest of the people. She knew there was no help coming for them. The mindset was not in helping others escape, but to simply escape when others failed; she had no shot at teaming up with any of them. She hoped Francis would be okay, but she knew there was no chance of that. The babies were bloodthirsty.

As she turned over her shoulder, she saw five of them rushing behind, eager to catch and kill anyone who faltered in their escape. Another scream filled the air as another soul was lost to the vicious jaws of the mutated monsters.

Jackie felt tears stinging her eyes as she tried to remember the movie she had just seen. The people were running from the killer geese; some got away, and others didn't, but that had only been a movie. It wasn't likely that those rules would have worked in real life. She pushed herself harder, her body beginning to tire as she cursed herself for not having spent more time in track and field while in high school.

Her parents always told her that sports were the way to go. Why had she focused her life on academics and art instead? A paintbrush would have done very little for her now as opposed to the ability to run the fuck away from killer mutant babies.

The people behind her started moving past her as Jackie faltered in her movements and tried to save her breath, only for a sudden weight on the back of her neck to force her to face-plant directly into the sidewalk. She screamed out in anguish and fear as a pair of gaping jaws latched onto the back of her head while teeth crushed through her cranium.

Within seconds, a series of sharp pains filled her legs as bites and chunks were stripped from them. She tried to scream, she tried to beg, she tried to pray, but all was futile as death came swiftly for her. The babies feasted on her warm body before giving chase after the growing crowd of pedestrians.

***

Rory drove the delivery truck along the wet road while trying to see through the fog that was filling the air. He hated foggy nights.

Malcolm was busy reading a magazine in the passenger seat as he ignored the sound of the siren that was filling the air. He sighed, doing his best to focus on the words that were coming off the page as he read them. The truck bumped along a pothole as he lost his place. Groaning in annoyance, he slapped the ends closed and threw the magazine on the dashboard.

Gripping the steering wheel, Rory looked over at him, "What?"

"Why are we going back to see the doc?"

"I already told you, I want to check on the babies."

"Doc Black said the babies would be fine. Hell, they're probably already speaking in different languages and walking upright," Malcolm replied, hoping his brother would fuck off with the urge to check on them. Rory had been unbearable the whole day as he thought about them. He looked at his brother. "Besides, we've got better things to do."

"Like what?"

"I don't know," Malcolm shrugged, "Maybe we can go catch a movie?"

"No, I want to make sure that man didn't harm the babies. I don't trust him."

"You don't trust anyone."

"I trust you," Rory replied, "for now, anyway."

"Fucking fine," Malcolm threw his hands up as they turned on the street heading for the warehouse. He knew that Rory would be a basket case until he saw that Black had followed through on his word. The plan was pretty sweet. Plus, the man was smart; he was the type with enough brains to help the world if he really wanted to.

He was smarter than them, anyway. Their parents had given them their own delivery company to create an income they could use for themselves; therefore, eliminating the need to rely on Daddy's fortune. However, the city was quite hellish, and the brothers had no clue about running a delivery service that could appease it.

Their company had died, and all they had left were their clothes, their truck, and their house. Still, they managed to make ends meet with the occasional odd job that was done through the contracts they got. Thankfully, Doc Black had been one guy they could rely on for a job.

Even if he didn't seem very happy with their time constraints.

Soon enough, they pulled up to where the warehouse once stood and were shocked to discover that it was nothing more than burning cinders of what it had once been. Rory parked the truck as he wrenched open the door to get out. Malcolm called after him to no avail as Rory walked toward the burning warehouse.

"Goddamnit," Malcolm got out after him and came up to the larger man, "What the fuck are you doing?"

"It's gone!"

"Clearly!" Malcolm exclaimed, "We can't do anything about it now!"

Rory looked up to see the fiery inferno that had gutted the warehouse. He didn't care about anything more than what might have happened to the babies. He screamed out, "Hello! Anyone!"

Malcolm watched as his brother screamed at a burning building and groaned. The larger man was lovable, but unfortunately, he was also a bit slow. Reaching up, he placed his hand on his brother's shoulder, patting softly as he whispered, "There's nobody there, Ror, I think they're gone."

"Gone where?"

"I don't want to take a guess," Malcolm replied while watching the fires continue to burn in the building. It looked like an accident had occurred, or arson, especially since this was a pretty bad part of the city. He could hear his brother sniffling as tears grew in the man's eyes. Shaking his head, Malcolm muttered, "Come on, let's get out of here before someone sees us."

Turning away, Malcolm stopped dead in his tracks as he looked down to see a bloodied corpse lying on the sidewalk. He froze. The corpse had been a man before being ravaged by some kind of animal. He looked like the victim of a wolf or a bear, or something else entirely. He shirked, "What the hell?"

Rory turned to his brother and saw the body, grimacing before looking away to see another body lying nearby. He gulped, "Mal, look!"

Slowly moving his head, Malcolm looked over to his brother and saw the other bodies that were lying on the street like some macabre decorations. Their bodies torn to shreds. Blood, guts, and gore speckled the sidewalks while shining in the moonlight above them; everything appeared so ghastly in their eyesight. Rory shivered, "What could have done this?"

"I suggest we don't find out," Malcolm replied before the pair quickly ran back to the delivery truck and got in, slamming the doors tight. Rory turned the key in the ignition to start up the truck while Malcolm opened the glovebox to retrieve the revolver they kept for potential trouble.

Malcolm gulped while hoisting the weapon in his hand and ensuring that it was loaded before looking out the window to see the corpses strewn along. He shuddered as they backed away from the curb and started back on the road, driving swiftly along as more corpses seemed to appear along the sidewalks beside them. Rory gripped the wheel tightly as his knuckles grew pale. He couldn't understand any of this.

His heart hurt for the babies, but now, he was afraid after seeing so many dead bodies. He turned to his brother, "Malcolm, what is going on?"

"I don't have a clue," Malcolm replied while gripping the pistol tightly in his right hand, "I'll tell you one thing. There's an animal loose and it's got rabies."

A rabid animal was the only thing that Malcolm could even begin to think of when he saw the carnage on the streets. There were bodies everywhere. People had been snuffed out in super violent ways, torn to shreds, and gutted like wild hogs. He could feel his heart racing as they pulled out onto the main road going through the district and breathed a sigh of panic.

The traffic was passing them as usual, the sirens were blasting heavily, and people seemed to be running along the sidewalks. Rory shook his head, "Mal, I'm afraid."

"You and I both," Malcolm whispered softly, "I got a bad feeling about all this."

"Me too."

"I don't think Doc Black's warehouse was an accident. I think he might have gotten carried away and done something bad."

"Like what?"

"I don't know," Malcolm shook his head, "But that guy was like a mad scientist, and you saw those packages we delivered. I think he might have made monsters."

"Monsters?"

"Yeah-," Malcolm froze in his seat as the pair watched a car careen into another before flipping over in front of them, and the driver's window busting open to reveal something crawling out of it. Rory released the steering wheel to rub his eyes and look clearly at what he was seeing.

Crawling out of the wrecked car was a toddler. Rory pressed the high beams to get a clearer view and saw that it looked more familiar than he thought. Malcolm gasped. The toddler had blood all over its gray body and seemed to be covered in sharp little rough patches; however, its jaws were large, and it had several sharp teeth extending from its maw.

"Oh no," Rory said before the toddler pounced up to the windshield of their truck and smashed its head through the thick glass, sending shards flying directly into the Suggs brothers. Malcolm pulled the trigger to shoot the monster, but was stopped as the beast snapped its jaws directly into the side of his neck. Rory screamed, "Malcolm! No!"

Malcolm swung his fists into the baby, scraping and shredding his knuckles in the process as he screamed out weakly, "Run, Rory, run!"

Frozen to his seat, Rory watched in horror as the toddler ripped into his brother's neck and tore loose the large artery that began to spray blood all over the inside of the cab. The toddler growled in a low guttural fashion while tearing hunks of wet meat from Malcolm, the man sluggishly moving to the side of the door before raising the barrel of the gun to the infant's head.

Rory shouted aloud as the gunshot filled the cab and deafened his ears. However, rather than being blanketed with brains from the toddler's head, the bullet had ricocheted off and blown through the passenger window. The toddler angrily continued in its efforts and, with a loud crackle, bit through Malcolm's spine.

Kicking open the door, Rory watched as his brother's head rolled off his body and blood sprayed out of the open neck stump. Turning away quickly, Rory leapt from the truck and started running across the street toward the other side, screaming in terror as he did.

The toddler, Romulus, lapped up the blood before turning to watch Rory running away. He wanted to give chase, but didn't. Something about the man seemed to stop him from giving chase.

However, another motorist came up alongside the truck to scream in annoyance, and within seconds, Romulus leapt from the cab through the open window to attack the screaming driver in the car.

CHAPTER TWENTY-EIGHT

Flames smoldered as smoke billowed high in the air of Winscott City, the skyscrapers outmatched by the massive stacks of smoke that seemed to dot the skyline. The city was under attack by the mutant monster babies, bodies were dropping like flies, and the city council had moved to the basement for safety.

Prescott Farthing looked at the other men sitting at the table as he rapped his fingertips on the surface, listening to the reports being broadcast on the news channel by the reporters. He sighed.

Twenty years ago, he'd been fighting in Vietnam and thought he'd seen it all. Now, he was the mayor of a city that was being engulfed in mayhem brought on by some kind of evil force he'd never considered possible.

Looking at one of the men, he spoke firmly, "What are the numbers?"

"We don't have a clear report," the man, Charles Kirk, replied. "We estimate thousands by now."

"Thousands," Prescott repeated, "How could it be thousands?"

Kirk, the police commissioner, simply shook his head. "I've been getting calls from the department. Every hour, we're learning about another series of attacks. The monsters are not slowing down."

"Monsters?"

"Sir?"

"Did you just say 'monsters'?"

"Yes, sir, I did," Kirk replied, holding steady in his response. Prescott nodded. "What do we know about these *monsters*?"

Kirk shrugged while fixing his necktie, "We know they're impenetrable against bullets. An officer attempted to fire on one, and the bullet bounced off like it was nothing; the officer was attacked shortly after. They appear to be in the form of human babies, infants, but they have been mutated."

"So, mutant monsters?"

"Sir?"

"We have mutant monsters attacking our city," Prescott growled in annoyance at the other man's incessant stupidity. There was no way this was possible. This was reality, not science fiction or the extreme horror books his wayward son brought home from the bookstore. He shook his head. "Horseshit."

"Sir, I know it sounds foolish, but I can only rely on the words of my men. We have to consider our options."

"Options," spat an older man sitting across from them. The man was rotund with silver hair and a burning cigarette dangling from his thin lips. The man shook his head, "We have only one option here. We have to activate the Winscott Special Defense Force. We're not playing games here; people are dying, and lives are at stake. If we don't activate the force, we can kiss our kids goodbye. Whatever's out there, whatever's taking out people, it's using deadly force, and we can't rely on the police to do their due diligence in stopping the threat. Hell, we can't rely on the police to maintain order regardless!"

Kirk rolled his eyes.

Colonel Ingram was a man always on a mission. He looked for any chance he could to stick his fat ass in other people's business. If it were up to him, Winscott wouldn't have a police department, just martial law that rained down fire on every miscreant and misdemeanor that jaywalked the street. Turning to Prescott, Kirk shook his head. "Mr. Mayor, we can't activate the defense force. The result would be catastrophic. We could see the death toll rise to tens of thousands when anyone and everyone is getting shot!"

"Nonsense," Colonel Ingram barked and smashed his cigarette out on the table. "Mayor, we're fucked either way. Remember, you were elected because you promised to crack down on crime. These monsters are causing crime to skyrocket more so than before Commissioner Kirk told the police to fuck around or whatever caused them to be useless. We can't let our citizens fend for themselves. We must stop it now!"

Prescott watched as Ingram slammed his fist on the table before another council member chimed in. "At least contain the monsters in less-populated areas before we deploy major weapons."

Before anyone else could speak, a sound of sobbing entered their ears as Prescott looked over to see one of the ward reps crying into a napkin. He tilted his head. "Mr. Gottschalk? What's wrong?"

Michael Gottschalk lowered the napkin he'd been sobbing on and spoke through his cracking voice. "I just got news. Lenore and Cara are dead. My wife and daughter are dead! I should have been there, goddamnit! I should have helped them!"

"Fuck me," Prescott groaned as he rubbed his forehead. The monsters had made it into the Pilsman district. They were now attacking outside of the poverty-stricken areas of the city. Kirk swallowed as Michael continued to sob into his napkin and angrily curse himself for wasting time with the council. Colonel Ingram shook his head in a mix of both sympathy for the man's loss and annoyance at the inept capability of the police to stop the situation from spreading.

Prescott sighed. "We have to stop them."

"Sir, please, be reasonable. If we deploy the defense force, we'll be left with a bigger mess than we have now," Kirk said, trying to sway the mayor's opinion. Ingram slammed his fist on the table again. "Shut the fuck up! Unless you want to go home and search through a bloodbath to find the pieces of your children, I demand you shut the fuck up!"

Kirk opened his mouth to speak before Michael cried out, "Stop! I vote for the defense force!"

Two other members chimed in to vote for the force as well. Ingram nodded. "I vote for the force."

Rubbing his furrowed brow, Prescott nodded, "In the time of such darkness, we must be the ones to bring the light; very well, deploy the defense force."

Ingram smiled as he walked toward the rotary phone against the wall and lifted the receiver before using his right index finger to turn the wheel on the numbers, sending out a call to the Winscott City arsenal. He sniffed. His men would be mavericks at ending the campaign of terror that the monsters had brought down on everyone.

Watch out, you little bastards, he thought, the big guns are coming to town.

CHAPTER TWENTY-NINE

Stephanie sat at a desk and tried to breathe slowly, still in a state of shock from having survived the attack. She felt her heart racing in her chest even though it had been more than an hour since the attack had occurred.

The dispatch control panel was lit up like a Christmas tree with people desperately calling for help against the nonstop massacres taking place all over the city. The other officers spoke amongst themselves while barricading the entrance of the station.

This was not right, she thought. They were supposed to serve and protect the people of the city. Yet, here they were, hiding like a bunch of chicken-shits while trying to save their own skin.

The reports of other officers on patrol had flooded in over the radio. The mutants were vicious, bloodthirsty, and couldn't be stopped with bullets. She had already seen it firsthand and knew, but thanks to the nonstop sexism that pervaded the office, it only mattered when a man saw it happen.

Figures, she thought.

Looking down at the desk, she was surprised as an older man's hand brought her a Styrofoam cup of steaming black coffee. She looked up to see Sgt. Collins before he sat in the chair facing her. He tilted his head with a pitiable look painted on his face. He shook his head. "How are you holding up?"

"Been better," she replied before raising the cup to her lips and hissing at the heat burning her tongue. Collins nodded as he sipped his own coffee and shrugged. "I don't blame you."

"Why'd you do it?"

"Huh?"

"Why did you give me the case?"

Collins sat back in the chair as he looked at her. She was focused on him with her eyes staring intently. She never stared at anyone. She usually avoided looking anyone in the eye directly. He clicked his tongue against his teeth and said, "Because I knew you'd find him."

Lowering the cup from her lips, Stephanie shook her head. "What?"

"That's right," Collins replied. "I knew if I gave you the case and jabbed you a bit about being so good at your job, you'd take it to heart. I spent a year trying to piece together anything I could about the perp and you usually solve shit in less than a month."

"So you weren't expecting me to fail?"

"Um, no?"

"Ah," Stephanie replied. First time she'd been wrong about something so trivial. Collins, however, tilted his head and cocked his eyebrow as he replied, "Did-Did you actually think I was setting you up for failure?"

"I did."

"Why would I do that?"

"Because you were jealous of my streak," she replied, "This department is run by men who all seem to have a problem with a woman doing anything more than washing the dishes."

"Valid point," Collins replied with a chuckle that quickly ended when he saw the lack of humor on her face. Shaking his head, he sighed. "Listen, West, I know this department is full of pigs, and I'm probably a big one, but I didn't expect you to fail. I knew you'd find the guy and bring him in. I knew I wouldn't get approval from the chief, so I pulled it anyway and handed it off. It might cost me my job, but I'll firmly take the blame for it. I wanted you to keep the streak and find the son of a bitch that's been killing everyone. Sounds like you had him dead to rights."

"I did," Stephanie nodded, "At least before…"

"Yeah." Collins finished his coffee. "Now, we have a bigger problem, and I've got a feeling that we won't be able to solve this one."

A loud explosion rocked the station from down the street, and the lights flickered as Stephanie looked around, anxiety hitting her with enough force to send her coffee to the floor. One of the officers started saying a Hail Mary aloud before being bitterly told to keep quiet.

Collins stood from his seat. "That sounded like the firehouse."

"Huh?"

"The fire department," Collins replied to Stephanie. "Whatever's out there is cutting off resources. Fires are going to burn, and nobody's going to put them out. The city is going to go down in flames by daybreak."

Stephanie felt her heart ready to burst through her chest as she gripped the desk with her hands. It was only a matter of time before the monsters came for the police. She didn't want to be there. She wanted to be back at home, asleep in bed, and most of all, she wanted her parents.

She held in her tears, unwilling to cry in front of everyone else as she tried to refocus her mind. It wasn't the end of the world, but it was close enough, and she didn't want to consider the outcome after everything was said and done.

Collins gulped as he pushed his hands in his trouser pockets. He'd been destined to retire in a year, and now, it was looking like retirement was coming quickly around the corner.

Suddenly, a banging came from the door of the station as someone pounded their fist on the door. Collins called out to the officers holding back the barricade, "Who is that?"

"Dunno," one of the officers called back before looking through the barricade towards the door. "A big guy!"

"Fuck," Collins whispered. He knew they were putting themselves in harm's way letting people into the station, but they also had a civic duty to let people in and save them from the streets. He had to make the choice, and he did. "Let him in!"

"Sergeant?"

"Let him the fuck in, now!"

One of the men groaned before pulling back the barricade of desks and filing cabinets as the man came barreling from outside. Stephanie took a look at the man.

He was large, probably six-foot-five, heavyset, and African-American. He had short hair. He had blood all over the denim jacket and pants he wore, but no visible wounds on his person. The man looked at them. "Officers, the city is under attack!"

"No joke," Collins replied, patting the man on the back as he attempted to calm him. "Take a breath, son."

The man heaved and puffed as he tried to relax. Finally, he nodded and took a sip of water from a cup that Collins had fetched. The older officer then said, "There, there; now, what's your name?"

"Rory Suggs," the man replied while finishing the small Styrofoam cup of water. Stephanie cocked her eyebrow before asking, "Any relation to Suggs Brothers Delivery Service?"

"The same," Rory replied. "Me and my brother," his voice trailed off, "Malcolm."

"I saw you guys a few nights ago." Stephanie crossed her arms. "Digging through trash cans."

"Yeah," Rory nodded while breathing slowly, "We were doing a job for a scientist. I gotta tell you, it's all part of what's going on outside."

"What do you mean?" Collins asked, "How's that?"

"We were helping a scientist with his experiment. He was trying to make some kind of serum to make babies smarter, to give them the ability to talk. We picked up and delivered everything he ordered from the docks: chemicals and some shark stuff. Finally, we were asked to find babies in trash cans, and we did it."

"Son, you know what you're saying sounds like a load of bullshit, right?" Collins smirked before Stephanie shushed him and nodded. "Continue?"

Swallowing, Rory said, "The babies had been left to die in trash cans all over the city. We got like twenty-two and brought them to him; he promised he'd take care of them all. He lied. We were driving on the highway and got attacked. It was one of the babies we brought him, except it was covered in scales and had mad sharp teeth. Malcolm, oh Malcolm, it got him…"

Rory's voice broke down as he started sobbing, and Collins paused before rubbing his back softly. Everyone had stopped to hear the story and turned to whisper to each other as Stephanie considered everything that had been said. Sure, it sounded like bullshit and Rory didn't seem to be the most believable person in the world, but she knew what she'd seen. Plus, the radios were reporting everything that would make it all correct.

She spoke softly to the man, doing her best not to sound cold. "I'm sorry for your loss. Who was the scientist?"

"Black," Rory replied through tears. "Doc Kermit Black. He said he would take care of the babies, and he turned them into monsters."

Collins nodded. He had heard of the Black family years earlier. They were successful, snobbish, and the patriarch had been a whackjob. He'd vaguely heard of Kermit, the black sheep of the Black family; once he'd been the subject of a very nasty article denouncing his scientific visions.

Seems like he'd managed to get something accomplished.

Stephanie shuddered as she considered the consequences of the experiment gone awry. Twenty-two mutant babies were one thing, but there was no way that they would have caused so much death and destruction on a mass scale. There had to be more than what was known.

However, there was no time to consider that; the focus now was on surviving the onslaught and conserving human life. She looked at Collins. "We need to alert the city council."

"Fat chance," Collins replied. "Once those sirens started, they goose-stepped it for the basement, and no calls were going to get in down there. We're on our own."

Soon enough, a radio broadcast came in as a female reporter started speaking. "We've just received word that Mayor Farthing has issued an order to activate the Winscott Defense Force to engage with the horde of monstrosities. The council estimates that it will be fully deployed within the hour. We reaffirm our previous order to stay indoors and do not venture into the streets, as the city is effectively entering a lockdown. We repeat, the city is locked down!"

Collins looked at Stephanie, "Hold on, it's going to get loud outside and we're going to be in for a long one."

Chapter Thirty

The Winscott City Arsenal was a large building located near the public gasworks in the city's industrial sector. It was a stone building that resembled a castle and had been constructed over a hundred years earlier, only to have fallen into disrepair as ordinances found fault with everything after a while.

The building housed a multitude of weapons for use against terrorists, both foreign and domestic, but thankfully, that proved to be a rarity.

Sitting in an office while watching a monitor, Lieutenant Aldridge spoke on the phone as he received a call from the head of the Defense Force, Colonel Sam Ingram. He nodded as he spoke. "Yes, sir. Yes, sir. Yes, sir."

Dropping the receiver once the call ended, he raised his hand and hit the large red button on the control panel that was built into the desk he sat at. The sound of a blaring alarm filled the building as red lights began to blink rapidly. The time had come to activate and deploy, so he hit the switch on the control panel to send the alerts to all members of the defense team.

Rising from his chair, he grabbed his ring of keys before vacating the office and heading down the corridor, where he was met by five other men in matching camouflage uniforms. One of them, Lieutenant Parker, looked at him. "Is this a drill?"

"Far from it," Aldridge replied, inserting the key into a large metal door that shifted weight once the key was turned. "This is the real deal."

"Fucking finally," another man replied as the group entered through the door and immediately made their way into a huge chamber that was lined with armored humvees and had dozens of rifles stored behind a large metal cage. Each of them started suiting up in combat gear, pulling on armored vests and helmets with clear visors for facial protection.

Aldridge pulled on his armored vest and fastened it into place before unlocking the door to the cage, issuing the weapons to each of the men. Soon enough, more people started coming through the door as their phones beeped with notifications and prepared them for the mission at hand. They knew their task was to take out enemy forces; however, they weren't informed about the current force they were facing.

Aldridge looked at them as they prepared themselves with the combat gear, and he raised a bullhorn to his lips. "Attention men, we have been activated to quell a potential wide-scale massacre that has fallen across the city. We have word that the enemy is nothing like anything we have faced before. They are not simply human. They are some form of hybrid mutants that are impossible to take out with regular ammunition. We will be facing creatures that may cause you to second-guess your actions; do not do it. We have orders to kill anything that poses a potential threat."

The men nodded in silence as they continued to dress themselves in the tactical gear, while others hurried to start up the Humvees, and others mounted the machine guns that were anchored to them. Aldridge swallowed before continuing, "The city is under lockdown. We have orders to kill anything that is not hidden indoors. If you think it may be a civilian, order it indoors, and if it refuses to comply, kill it. Colonel Ingram has given us full right to use whatever force is necessary in saving the city from the invasive mutant hybrids."

The soldiers finished their preparation before getting aboard the armored Humvees to start out of the facility and head towards the city. Aldridge lowered the bullhorn and set it aside before grasping the M16 that he'd been eyeing the entire time. Once he had it on himself, he watched the men go into fight mode. They were each ready for the chance to do their job.

As it turned out, fifty men sitting in wait for something to happen day-in and day-out was damned irritating. More men would be arriving soon, and volunteers from throughout the city would be joining them within the hour. The full force would be hundreds, but he didn't expect that they would need all of them for the activity at hand.

Parker approached Aldridge and spoke, "Sir, what's our time of departure?"

"We'll depart at 0400 and be in the muck within minutes—the Colonel relayed that the enemy forces have gotten as far as Pilsman. We'll have to hunker down and hit them hard, don't be afraid to throw everything you've got at the little bastards."

"Yes, sir."

Aldridge looked down at his watch as he counted the minutes. *Soon*, he thought, *soon they'd be heroes.*

***

After breaking through the chain link fence that was topped with barbed wire outside of the arsenal building, Mr. Giggles looked up at the heavy metal doors that blocked the entrance and turned to the monster newborns that had followed after him. He hissed at them as they watched him, their dark eyes staring while growls of hunger emanated from their bellies.

Raising his right clawed hand, he motioned toward the large windows that showed red lights flickering from within. The newborns readied in their stance as their leader sprang forward and propelled his head to crash through the window, bursting it open as the others followed after.

The five little mutant monsters moved together in a pack as they scampered through the corridors of the building. Mr. Giggles broke off to go toward a staircase while the others made their way to the sound of people talking.

Lights flickered constantly, and the alarms continued to buzz through the facility as the newborns crashed through each door to find the source of the communication they were hearing. The sound of someone speaking through a loud bullhorn acted as a clear indicator that there was someone else in the building.

Finally, one of them thrust himself forward to send a door off its hinges and onto the metal floor.

Aldridge and Parker looked up to see what had knocked the door to the floor. His brown eyes widened as he took note of four infants, each no bigger than a loaf of bread.

Their skin was gray and rough, while their mouths were pulled into gaping jaws full of gleaming teeth.

Aldridge immediately raised his M16 and jerked his finger back on the trigger, watching as the large rounds came firing out of the barrel of the rifle toward the encroaching hybrid monsters. The other soldiers had turned by this point to see what was being shot at.

They gasped in shock as Parker quickly fell back to the floor, struck in the face by a bullet that had bounced off the skull of an infant. Aldridge looked down at Parker and ceased pulling the trigger. "Shit, Parker! Parker!"

Parker's face stared up at the ceiling of the chamber while blood poured freely from the gaping hole in his cheek. Before he could turn back, Aldridge was brought to the floor by two of the infants who had leapt onto his torso. He called out to the men, ordering them to fire, to do anything they could to save themselves.

One soldier turned the machine gun on a Humvee he was manning and pulled the trigger, sending loud bursts of firepower toward the mutants. The babies were quickly scampering around the floor while leaping up to attack the other men. The large bullets bounced off their flesh to fly into everything else, marking the walls, floor, and vehicles with bullet holes. He continued firing until a large pair of jaws flung into his face and ripped his head clear off his neck, sending a geyser of bright red blood into the air that rained down on everyone else.

More men yelled out in terror and fear as they were mauled by the newborns ripping their limbs from their bodies, while others watched their innards fall from the holes ripped in their torsos. One soldier, feeling the infants tearing him apart from the waist, reached into his combat vest and pulled a grenade.

He primed it before rolling it towards the others that were being ripped to shreds by the monsters. The grenade rolled until it stopped and lay still; the man simply closed his eyes in preparation for what would happen next.

The grenade ignited and exploded, sending a massive fireball within the enclosed chamber. Within seconds, the force ripped through the facility and caught aflame the ammunition that had been stored on the ground floor, causing an even larger explosion to overtake the grounds of the arsenal.

***

Within the basement of the arsenal, Mr. Giggles listened as the top level of the building was destroyed by the blast of a grenade. He giggled to himself, earning a bit of surprise that he'd still managed to return to his old self.

Looking around the massive underground area, his eyes fixated on everything that had been kept under supreme lock and key. There were bombs. Enough explosives to level an island or most of the city itself. It was perfect. The perfect means to an end.

Crawling along the floor, Mr. Giggles continued to move along until he stopped at a large missile that was planted on a pair of holders. They were heavy and anchored to the floor, holding up the massive weapon that packed enough punch to be horrific to the innocent civilian.

It was just too perfect.

Climbing up on the table that housed the control panel under a cover of heavy glass, Mr. Giggles brought his face down into the glass and shattered it, revealing the controls to his clawed fingers. Pressing the buttons as they lit up, he thought about the amount of pain and chaos that would be unleashed as he worked each switch into its upright position and watched as lights began to hum throughout the area.

Looking up to the side of the wall, Mr. Giggles noticed a key dangling from the metal chain it was attached to. He marveled at it before climbing up to rip it from the wall and held it in his hand. The control panel had an ignition next to a large, round, green button.

Jamming the key into the ignition and turning it, he watched as the button lit up. The sounds of humming and whirring were filling the entire underground chamber now as he pondered the next move to make. His intelligence dictated that the button would launch the missile, but there was no guarantee.

At any rate, it would set something off, and that would cause the missile to ignite. The resultant explosion would be absolutely breathtaking to watch. It would be massive and terrifying, possibly even world-ending. No, he realized, the missile was not nuclear and it wouldn't end everything on the planet, but it would do substantial harm to the city itself.

The city.

Winscott City.

He'd been born here. He'd nearly died here. The city was dying just as he was, if only figuratively speaking. He was still a toddler and still had a lot of life to live before death took him, but the city had run its course. It had failed its people just as it had failed him. He couldn't allow it to continue.

It was an act of mercy that the city didn't deserve.

He slammed his clawed hand on the button and watched as a timer appeared on the control panel, bright red numbers counting down from 60 seconds. He giggled harder as he watched the numbers count backward. It wouldn't be long.

And yet, it would be too long in his opinion.

Chapter Thirty-One

Stephanie, Collins, and Rory sat waiting for the response of the city's defense force. They expected bombs to fall and explosions to rip apart everything in the fight against the mutant monsters.

Rory looked at them and shook his head. "I never would have taken part in this if I'd known that Doctor Black was going to turn the babies into monsters."

Collins looked up at him and shook his head too. "Well, give a maniac the tools and he'll make monsters."

Another officer chuckled from afar before being told to shut up. The sound of smaller explosions filled the air as Stephanie looked over at Collins. "Is that them?"

"No," Collins shook his head, "The defense force is going to throw everything they've got at the monsters. If it gets too bad, they'll use the big one."

"Big one?'

"Yeah." Collins nodded. "There's a big bomb at the arsenal. A while back, Mayor Cambridge ordered the arsenal to house a missile for the chance of a last stand against the Russians. He was more paranoid than Mayor Farthing is, and as far as I know, it's still down there."

Stephanie shuddered at the idea that there was a massive bomb in the city and she had gone her whole life never knowing about it. She looked at him. "How do you know?"

"Because I was part of the defense force when I was younger. I helped them bring it in. Don't worry about it, I'm sure that there's no chance they'll be using it."

"If you're sure."

"I am," Collins replied, matter-of-factly. "They'll resort to grenades and rocket launchers if they need to use any explosives."

It wasn't much of a relief to think that everything would be rocked to pieces by explosives when she eventually left the station. The idea that the city had been relatively normal only hours earlier was haunting to her.

Rory swallowed. "Are we going to be safe here?"

"Safer than out there," Stephanie replied as Collins nodded. "Yeah, I think we'll be fine," and looked to see officers heading toward the basement. "Still, we might need to head to the cellar."

Stephanie nodded before grabbing her purse and getting out of her chair, waiting for Collins and Rory to start toward the cellar. It was under the building and didn't have much use other than storage for cold-case files from decades earlier, files that probably had fallen prey to rats by that point.

Collins stood up with a sigh and patted Rory's back. "C'mon, we better get down there."

The others started following quickly as the group made their way from the lobby and headed for the stairwell that led down to the basement, already seeing that a majority of them had reached the area. It was dark and cramped, but it would protect if an explosive hit the building itself.

The last thing Collins wanted was for any of them to die. Already, there had been multiple deaths among the patrolmen, and it was harrowing to consider the families that would be missing their loved ones. But that wasn't something to consider for the time.

Stephanie rested against one of the walls as Rory and Collins moved beside her. Collins looked down at her, his eyes marveling at her figure in the catsuit. He'd never really had the chance to check her out before, and since a little levity was needed, he took the moment to say, "You look really good tonight."

The woman cocked her eyebrow at him, "Um, thanks?"

"Just saying." Collins chuckled. "You chose the right outfit to go undercover in."

"Yeah," Stephanie simply muttered as she thought back to the failed operation. She didn't worry anymore about getting busted over going undercover without approval or backup; now, she worried about the chance that the man might not have even been the Foot Carver. It was a nagging feeling that seemed to gnaw away at her.

The whole city was under attack by mutant monster hybrid babies, and she was kicking herself over failing to capture a serial killer who, for all she knew, had already fallen prey to the monsters. She hated the way her mind worked.

She could remember details and facts, but she couldn't get herself to focus on the important things that mattered: like having a life, or pursuing a relationship, or even enjoying the little things that existed outside of work.

Like having a drink with friends or even having friends.

Friends. She sighed. The idea of friends was almost foreign to her. She couldn't ever consider the notion when she had done nothing but work most of her life. Maybe it would have been something to focus on when she was younger.

She looked at Collins while thinking carefully to choose her words and whispered, "Thank you for believing in me."

"I always have," Collins replied while smiling at her. She couldn't help but feel a connection to him, despite the times he'd been cantankerous toward her in the past. Perhaps it was just his way. She knew she wasn't much better when it came to being social or even easy to work with. She was seeing him in a new light that was really interesting, if not somewhat scary.

He was like a father, in a fucked-up kind of way, especially since she hadn't had a father since hers was taken from her. She swallowed. She needed to get off the topic. They were coworkers, and that was that, no ifs, ands, or buts about it. Turning to look down at the floor, she considered her options if they survived the night.

She was going to turn in her badge and go back to school, maybe even pursue that novel she'd been wanting to write for the longest time. It was something new. She hated it. She hated the idea of breaking her routines and compulsions, but after so long in a job she was growing to hate, it might have been time to start over.

She looked back toward Collins. "What time is it?"

Collins looked at his watch, ignoring the fact that Stephanie had her own on her wrist, before replying, "Three-fifty-eight."

They'd start soon. Their deployment was stated to begin at four in the morning, and there would be a lot of noise above them, she thought. She reached up to hold her ears as Rory saw her and did the same, unsure of what he was going to hear. He knew, however, that it wasn't going to be good.

Looking at the two before turning to look up at everyone else in the basement, Collins closed his eyes before opening them softly. It was impossible to consider what was going on in the streets above. The people were being attacked and ripped to pieces by the monsters while they all just sat in wait for the defense force to begin an assault on everything.

This was the kind of stuff he'd seen in a horror film. The wait was worse than the knowing, and it seemed to get worse with each passing second.

Suddenly, a massive booming sound filled the air as Collins reached up to grip his ears and close them as the entire basement shook apart. The shelves of books fell over onto each other, one man being trapped as a shelf collapsed onto his body and crushed him under boxes of files and rat shit. The lights flickered before going out and throwing everything into pitch black darkness.

Stephanie slid down to the base of the wall as she cried out, doing her best to hold her ears shut and stop the anxiety from crushing her lungs within. She shook against herself as another massive boom blasted from across the city above them and forced everyone to scream out in fear.

Collins knew the sound was not a simple grenade or rocket; it was something else. Something much worse. Survival was going to be very hard to ensure if he was correct in his assumption.

He hoped he wasn't.

Chapter Thirty-Two

The seconds continued to count down with each passing moment as Mr. Giggles watched intently. Thirty seconds to total destruction, and he was giggling more with each change of the numbers. It was absolutely breathtaking as he felt himself getting excited at the big boom.

Once the counter hit twenty-five, he turned to crawl down from the control panel and scampered along the floor toward the door, his barnacle-laden skin cramping along the white floor as he reached the open door. Pushing through, he started up the stairs toward the door leading to the corridor.

He didn't expect to get out in time.

Bullets bounced off of him like nothing more than toothpicks, but a massive explosion would take him out, and he knew there was little to no chance of surviving it. However, that didn't matter, the city itself would be fucked. It made sense to him that he would die with it.

However, he wanted to see the city go up in flames and smolder like the end of a burning cigarette. It would be a fun event to witness. His heart raced in his small chest as he crawled rapidly up the stairs toward the ground level of the facility. He moved swiftly as he entered the doorway.

Smoke billowed heavily from the fires that had torn through the ground-level and around him, he saw the debris of the explosion that the grenade had set off. Nobody could have survived it. The entire arsenal went up in smoke.

Turning to his right, he continued toward the main entrance while rushing through the fires that simmered hot in his vicinity. The smoke choked his nose and burned his eyes as he threw his energy into the rush toward the entrance. He had to make it.

He wanted to more than anything else.

The countdown continued in his head. He could almost see it reach ten seconds as he made his way toward the last hall and the main door of the building. The roof had fallen through, and fiery debris blocked his egress, but he ran for it regardless.

A thought crossed his mind that he should have left sooner, but he'd hoped twenty-five seconds would be long enough to make it out of the facility for a clear view of the destruction. Unfortunately, he'd underestimated the damage done to the building as he realized there was no chance of getting out before the explosion.

Mr. Giggles could only watch the fires burning around him as he let out a roar of giggles that peppered through the crackling flames. He'd beaten himself in the process. He wouldn't get to see the city be destroyed, but he'd get to see the white flash of death before everyone else.

And it would be much better in retrospect.

The countdown finished in the basement of the facility as the missile was triggered within its shell, and the igniting fire hit the high-powered explosives within, resulting in an immediate chain reaction that ripped through the hard metal casing of the bomb. The fires filled it as it exploded.

Mr. Giggles heard the explosion rumbling louder than any other sound as it deafened him before everything around him grew blindingly white. He giggled hard as the entire building went up in an enormous fire. The explosion propelled him through the air as the ground lifted from the mighty force below and sent his fiery body shooting high into the clouds of the early morning sky.

***

Across from the now leveled industrial district, a homeless vagrant looked out in shock as the ground below his feet shook and a blanket of flames came rushing toward him. He turned quickly to run as fast as he could, despite his old body not pushing him very far.

The other pedestrians ran as fast as they could upon seeing the approaching wave of roaring fire that blew out at them. The ground began to lift and burst open as cars swerved from the road to fall into the chasm. The fires burst forward at breakneck speeds as they engulfed the vagrant and the hundreds of others who were attempting to outrun them.

Buildings on the block crumbled as their foundations shattered, and the fires blew out the windows, sending glass into the broken streets. One by one, they toppled over to collapse into the ground and pancake those who weren't instantly immolated by the flames that continued to push out through the districts of the city.

The fire surged through the air as it continued to gain ground and move with unmerciful haste upon the fleeing people attempting to save themselves. Apartment complexes and slums burst into massive explosions as bodies rained down from their windows, collapsing into the ground in puddles of blood and gore.

Cars swerved and collided into each other as they attempted to outrun the destruction that had no end in sight. Crashing open, the ground continued to burst into a massive chasm that flew directly through the middle of the city, bringing down skyscrapers as they fell into others and were blanketed by the fires of the explosion.

***

Romulus looked out from the body he'd been busy tearing through and saw the clouds of intense heat and yellow flame rushing his way. He let out a growl of panic before the flames blasted past him, and his body was immersed in hellish fire, instantly falling, charring to nothing more than a pile of burnt ash.

***

Feeling the basement shaking enough to knock coffee cups from the table and shatter on the floor, Mayor Farthing looked at Colonel Ingram. "Colonel! What is the meaning of this?"

"Someone must have detonated *The Hammer*," Colonel Ingram exclaimed as the sound of city hall collapsing above them shook the basement. Commissioner Kirk looked at him. "You don't mean?"

"That's right," Ingram replied as his cigarette fell from his lips. "The last resort."

"Impossible," Mayor Farthing shook his head. "It hasn't been operational since Mayor Oswell! He saw to it that Cambridge's paranoid bluff was dismantled."

Ingram sighed. He wished he could tell the mayor that they'd followed through and had it dismantled, just as he had told the last mayor, but unfortunately, that'd be a lie. And he wasn't itching to go to his maker with another lie on his life's rap sheet. He shook his head. "It was never dismantled. It's been operational since day one, and now, we're paying for it."

Farthing growled and slammed his fist on the desk. "That's it! Colonel, you're fired! You're all fired!"

The walls ripped apart instantly as the ceiling collapsed upon everyone, and within minutes, fires poured in from above to bathe everyone in a burning flame that forced them all to sizzle beyond a crisp. Mayor Farthing screamed out in jarring anger until his flesh melted from his skeleton, and he was silenced by the roaring flames.

***

Winscott City continued to be rocked as the ground split open wider throughout the middle of it, and several more chasms broke open like branches leading from the main trunk of the destruction.

Looking out the window from her bedroom, Sally's heart sank in her chest as she saw the ocean of fire bursting through the city toward her neighborhood. She'd been up all night waiting for Henry to return home.

He'd left his man cave door open, and she'd broken the cardinal rule of never going in it. She found everything: the shoes, the dismembered feet, breasts, and other grotesque trophies he'd kept. She even found an old scrapbook containing the articles he'd cut from the newspapers that covered his crimes.

At first, she didn't want to believe that her husband was the Winscott Foot Carver. She *couldn't* believe it. The kids already had it hard enough living in the city that was full of criminals and psychotics, but the fact that their father was one of them would destroy their trust in humanity; even at such a young age, it would ruin their lives before they had a chance to live them.

Unfortunately, as she saw the fires grow closer, she knew their lives were already destroyed, as was hers. She didn't care if Henry came home, and she didn't care if he was safe from the fires; she just didn't care.

Rushing from her bedroom, she made her way to the kids' room and saw Richard and Liz fast asleep in the bed they shared. They were adorable when they slept. They were adorable when they were awake, too.

A tear ran down her cheek as she crawled beside them before flinging her arm around them both. They shuddered slightly from the interruption to their sleep, but didn't wake. She whispered to them softly, knowing her words would enter their ears even if they didn't wake. "I love you both. I'm sorry."

There was nothing she could do. The explosions were starting to fill the air outside the house, and she could see the glow of flames in the window next to their bed. She could only give them the love that they deserved, just as she always did, but now for the last time.

She closed her eyes as the fires broke through the walls of the house and incinerated everything.

***

The newborns continued on their rampage throughout the city, attacking and mauling everyone they could as their little hearts were hell-bent on total annihilation of society. Screams continued to fill the streets as the ground beneath them ripped asunder and created massive burrows that opened to reveal fires from ignited gases blazing out of them.

Looking around, the newborns growled and hissed at each other as the blanket of flames pursued them and within minutes, burned straight through them all. The fires continued on the warpath as more buildings fell like blasting done by a bomb-happy construction team.

The buildings fell after they exploded, raining glass, debris, and fiery remains down on the people below. One by one, pedestrians and monsters alike were struck by the sea of heat that engulfed most of the city. Winscott City continued to fall as the blast ignited through the gas lines and broke through the heavy concrete to rip apart decades-old buildings.

Fires rampaged across, as all objects in sight were taken out in smoldering heat. The smoke of the rising flames grew in mass until it lifted like a funnel over the top of the destroyed city.

Sitting up in his bed in the Everett district across the river, Peter McEntire looked out at the glowing monstrosity that had been a city before he'd gone to sleep. He'd come to Winscott on business, and now, he had a feeling that the business meeting was canceled.

The building it was set up in, was falling to the ground below as he watched from afar. Clearing his throat, he slowly turned to the phone by his bedside and picked up the receiver before dialing the numbers for his home back in Benton. The phone rang a few times before someone finally answered, "Hello?"

"Barb, I'm coming home. This city is a hell-hole."

"Don't you have a meeting tomorrow?"

"Well," he turned to look out the window and saw the burning remnants of the building before licking his lips. "I'm pretty sure I'm unemployed."

***

Hours passed as Stephanie and the other officers remained steadfast in the basement of the police station.

The walls had cracked and torn, but hadn't shattered like they thought they would.

Thankfully, the station had been built as one of the safest places in the city by Mayor Cambridge back in the 70s.

Stephanie opened her eyes slowly as she realized she'd been resting her head against Collins' shoulder with her legs spread out on the floor. She turned to look at him, seeing his head lowered while he slept as peacefully as he could. She yawned slightly as she looked around to see the other officers, some awake and some asleep, while others tended to the injured men who had been smashed by the shelves.

She turned to her left to see Rory trying to sleep as well.

Yawning a bit more, she felt the urge to light up a cig and sip some coffee, regardless of whether this was heaven or hell. She didn't believe in either, but it was something that made her laugh despite the situation. Raising slowly, she did her best to avoid jostling Collins despite doing so anyway.

The older man looked up quickly with his eyes open before looking up at her. She whispered, "Sorry."

"It's fine," he replied as he slowly pushed himself up and sighed in pain from having been sitting in an uncomfortable position for so long. He wasn't a young man anymore. Sitting for long hours against a wall was not something he could do as well as he had in his youth, no matter what he told himself. Looking around, he called out, "Everyone okay?'

"Yeah. Sure. Yep. Fuck do you think?" came the mixed responses from the other officers that were still awake. He heard others but didn't register them as he turned to Stephanie. "So, looks like we survived, hard as it may seem."

"Yeah," she nodded, "But how bad do you expect the city to be?"

"Oh, I have no doubt it's going to be a nightmare getting home."

"Humor?"

"Eh," Collins shrugged. "Gotta find something to laugh about."

Stephanie shook her head in annoyance. There was nothing funny about any of this. The whole thing had been something straight out of a nightmare. She turned to look down at Rory and shook his shoulder, jarring him from sleep. He looked up. "What happened?"

"It's okay, you're okay, come on." She offered her hand, which he took as she heaved and pulled the tall man to his feet. He nodded his thanks to her before they turned to move for the stairs leading to the top of the ground level.

Collins coughed slightly as he approached the staircase and turned to everyone else. "I'll go check it out."

"Why you?" another officer asked before he shrugged. "Because I volunteered. Anyone else want to volunteer?"

The others quickly waved their hands in dismissal and shook their heads, none too eager to see what was left of the city, nor the shock of seeing the destruction that had befallen everything. Collins gave an annoyed smirk. "That's what I thought."

Annoyed at the others, Stephanie followed behind him as they made their way up the staircase toward the ground floor of the station. Collins gripped the door handle and hesitated before turning to look at Stephanie. "There could be blowback, be careful."

"Noted," she replied dryly as Collins nodded and twisted the door handle to open the door for them. To their surprise, the door opened easily as he pulled it open wide and started through it. Stephanie followed slowly behind him as they made their way out of the basement and through what was left of the building.

She gasped.

Everywhere she looked was debris, smoldering and smoking, as the entire building had been blown apart. The desks, tables, files, and other bits were scattered about as the morning sunlight peered from above. Collins walked through the debris out toward the sidewalk and shook his head. "God damn."

Stephanie followed suit before pausing. The city had been leveled to the point that it looked flat, with only the buildings in their area still standing with some ease. The district had been too far for the flames to travel as they had through the others.

It was hardly a comforting thought as she realized almost all of the city had been completely obliterated into nothing more than fiery death. The flames continued to burn as the smoke filled the morning sky and the air was thick with the pungent fumes of burning flesh, trash, and old buildings; her eyes hurt as she saw how powerful the big bomb had been in regards to everything.

Looking across the way, Stephanie saw the roads had been uplifted and broken through by the flaming destruction from beneath the ground. Hell had visited the city and left absolute chaos in its wake, resulting in a death toll of at least millions. It was a nightmare she'd been dreading, and yet, she was still shocked to see it come to life.

The air was soon cut through by the sound of the other officers as they made their way into the street. Their hearts sank and their eyes welled with tears as the thought of their families dying brutally filled their minds. Rory looked around as he heard other moans and cries for help emanate from the areas of destruction.

Collins rolled up his sleeves as he turned to Stephanie. "Well, I guess we'd better do the right thing and find survivors."

Stephanie gave a small, if not unneeded, smile and nodded, "Probably a good idea."

"Good. Glad I have your approval," Collins quipped and turned to the others to start forming a team to find survivors and help anyone they could. Stephanie scowled at him from behind his back. He was such a dick. She thought she'd started seeing him in a new light just hours earlier, but fuck that noise.

Collins was going to be a dick no matter how she thought of him. The other officers weren't going to be that much better either. The city was destroyed, people were dead, and the monsters had been defeated at the cost of everything else. It made sense.

Winscott was a cursed city that had saved itself by destroying itself, like some fucked-up poetic justice.

She hated to admit it, but all in all, this event had made her upcoming resignation much easier. She'd just hold off until after the survivors were rounded up.

It might take more than a few months, and she might change her mind before then, but all in good time.

EPILOGUE

Lounging on a chair in front of a roaring blue ocean, Crystal Cook relaxed. The breath of fresh air entering her nostrils before leaving her mouth was almost like a narcotic.

Running a publishing house in Winscott City was no picnic. The books she read daily were usually good, but there were too many freaks out there trying to put out books about off-the-wall bonkers bullshit. Plus, the city itself was a giant hassle from hell.

She'd opted for a vacation on Creechmore Island and bought the tickets a year in advance.

It was a nice little resort that presented all the amenities she liked and plenty of other vacationers who kept to themselves, a pleasant little trip away from the hustle and bustle of the city. She'd kept the radio off and did everything she could to avoid going back to her hotel room; no, she was going to enjoy the beach for all its worth.

Her eyes were closed as she lay back in the chair. Her tanned skin bathed in the sunlight as her long legs stretched out in the sand. Better living was only found in a magazine at the dirty supermarket bookshelf, and she was going to enjoy it for as long as she could.

She'd get drunk out of a cup fashioned from a coconut with the little umbrella, perhaps get a new tattoo to add to her multiple others, and after all was said and done, she'd book her flight back to the city to see what had changed while she was gone.

Regardless, she didn't want to think of what she would do and wanted to focus on what she was doing.

Breathe in and breathe out, she thought. *Just enjoy the sound of the ocean waves as they collided with the beach in front of you. It's like a dream come true. Island living is where it's at.* She didn't even bother to call into the office and check how everything was going.

Books were being sold, and people were making money; that was pretty much the highlight of the publishing world.

The gnawing feeling of a mountain of manuscripts on her desk kept her from truly relaxing as she reached down to grasp her glass of wine. She needed a sip—nothing like getting a bit smashed on the beach to ensure it was a good time.

Reaching down, she felt her towel, her book that she'd brought along to read, and finally, something that seemed coarse. *Sand*, she thought, *it's the beach after all.*

Raising her hand to look as she opened her eyes, she furrowed her brow at the black ash that caked her fingertips. She'd expected to see dirt, but not ash. She whispered, "The fuck?"

Raising herself, she turned to look down before her eyes grew wide at the sight of a creature covered in charred skin lying next to her chair. The creature turned to look up at her with its wide eyes and released a quick giggle from its wide mouth. No sooner than it giggled, the monster leaped up to latch its teeth onto her head, crushing down with its jaws.

Crystal screamed out as she fell from her chair onto the soft sandy beach. The monster ripped and jerked its head as rows of jagged teeth proceeded to tear a massive section of her head off. The blood burst forth from the open crater as her brain was exposed through the skull. The monster spat out the bite before turning to sink its shark-like jaws into her ribcage and tear through her flesh, breaking the ribs to lap up her juicy organs.

Her blood poured out rapidly as the sand around her grew red with her fluids. Her eyes stared out into the distance as her body was mauled and torn by the monster that consumed her. It gulped down her flesh and muscle as it gorged itself.

Mr. Giggles finished slurping through her body as he looked around the beach, noticing the clear blue ocean rushing back and forth on the sandy shoals. He giggled as he considered the fact that he'd survived the explosion of the city. He hadn't gotten to see it except for glimpses as he floated away on the surface of the water.

His skin was charred, burnt to a flaking crisp, yet he could feel it beginning to renew itself thanks to the water. The good doctor really didn't know what he was doing when he created the serum. Thankfully, that problem had been solved directly, and while the others were lost in the explosion, Mr. Giggles was far from done.

The city had paid for abandoning him and his horde, but the world was still busy doing the same thing. One city mattered little in the grand scheme of things, and he still had nothing but energy to fuel his burning desires for vengeance.

His black, lifeless eyes could almost see the deaths and carnage he'd cause along the way. The bodies of the worms dying on their backs as they fell to his hunger was something that forced his heart to beat with a rush of pure joy.

Scampering from the body of the publisher, he slowly crawled along the beach as his charred skin pulled from his body along the sand and his eyes fixated on something further along the island: a building.

It was a large building with smaller ones nearby. They were white, glowing from the sunlight, with people milling about in vacation wear. All of them ranged from fat to thin to athletic, all were laughing or talking, and all of them were prime targets.

The resort was built for people to get away from their lives and try to focus on relaxation and rest. It was a place meant to be a getaway from the stress and psychotic bullshit found in a big city. However, the resort was about to become something that would only be found in a nightmare.

It was full of people trying to shed the responsibilities of their lives for just a day or a week or even a month. Everyone deserves at least one vacation to enjoy their lives, regardless of whether it matters.

Mr. Giggles could already taste their blood as he started crawling toward the resort. It was going to be a bloodbath, and he was ready to indulge himself, especially since he still had a full life ahead of him.

He giggled at the thought of it.

He was going to enjoy every day of it, regardless of who suffered in the process.

ABOUT THE AUTHOR

Jerry Blaze is an international bestselling author of Horror and Bizarro fiction.

After achieving success in the erotic market, Jerry decided to undertake Extreme Horror/Splatterpunk/Bizarro fiction writing and released several books. Some of his books have been bestsellers on Amazon. He has been awarded the 2025 Golden Wizard Book Prize and the Literary Titan award.

Jerry is a fan of Grindhouse and exploitation films from the 70s and 80s, often modeling his work on them. He currently lives in the American Midwest, but travels often to get inspiration or to run away from angry mobs.

www.ingramcontent.com/pod-product-compliance
Lightning Source LLC
Chambersburg PA
CBHW071726190726
48292CB00003B/629